"Kissing Was An Excellent Discovery,"

Dakota observed, appearing extremely proud of himself. "We're moving closer to the time of joining."

"No, we're not," Kathy said, her voice rising. "Yes, okay, I want you, I want to join with you. It's called making love, if the proper emotions are involved. But it isn't going to happen between us, Dakota."

"Why not?"

She folded her arms over her breasts. "Listen to me carefully. I do *not* take the act of making love lightly."

"Nor do I."

"Fine. Then you should be able to understand that it's too risky. What if I... Darn it, what if I fall in love with you and then you zoom back to 1877?"

Dear Reader,

It's the **CELEBRATION 1000** moment you've all been waiting for, the publication of Silhouette Desire #1000! As promised, it's a very special MAN OF THE MONTH by Diana Palmer called *Man of Ice*. Diana was one of the very first Silhouette Desire writers, and her many wonderful contributions to the line have made her one of our most beloved authors. This story is sure to make its way to your shelf of "keepers."

But that's not all! Don't miss *Baby Dreams,* the first book in a wonderful new series, THE BABY SHOWER, by Raye Morgan. Award-winning author Jennifer Greene also starts a new miniseries, THE STANFORD SISTERS, with the delightful *The Unwilling Bride*. For something a little different, take a peek at Joan Elliott Pickart's *Apache Dream Bride*. And the fun keeps on coming with Judith McWilliams's *Instant Husband,* the latest in THE WEDDING NIGHT series. Our Debut Author promotion introduces you to Amanda Kramer, author of the charmingly sexy *Baby Bonus*.

And you'll be excited to know that there's more **CELEBRATION 1000** next month, as the party continues with six more scintillating love stories, including *The Accidental Bodyguard,* a MAN OF THE MONTH from Ann Major.

Silhouette Desire—the passion continues! Enjoy!

Lucia Macro

Senior Editor

Please address questions and book requests to:
Silhouette Reader Service
U.S.: 3010 Walden Ave., P.O. Box 1325, Buffalo, NY 14269
Canadian: P.O. Box 609, Fort Erie, Ont. L2A 5X3

JOAN ELLIOTT PICKART

APACHE DREAM BRIDE

SILHOUETTE *Desire*®

Published by Silhouette Books

America's Publisher of Contemporary Romance

For Herm Harrison
Professional Football Player!
Super Star!
Hero!
But most of all…my friend.

 SILHOUETTE BOOKS

ISBN 0-373-75999-1

APACHE DREAM BRIDE

This edition published by arrangement with Harlequin Books S.A.

® and TM are trademarks of Harlequin Books S.A., used under license.
Trademarks indicated with ® are registered in the United States Patent
and Trademark Office, the Canadian Trade Marks Office and in other
countries.

Printed in U.S.A.

Books by Joan Elliott Pickart

Silhouette Desire

*Angels and Elves #961
Apache Dream Bride #999

Silhouette Special Edition

*Friends, Lovers...and Babies! #1011
*The Father of Her Child #1025

*The Baby Bet

Previously published under the pseudonym Robin Elliott

Silhouette Desire

Call It Love #213
To Have It All #237
Picture of Love #261
Pennies in the Fountain #275
Dawn's Gifts #303
Brooke's Chance #323
Betting Man #344
Silver Sands #362
Lost and Found #384
Out of the Cold #440
Sophie's Attic #725
Not Just Another Perfect Wife #818
Haven's Call #859

Silhouette Special Edition

Rancher's Heaven #909
Mother at Heart #968

Silhouette Intimate Moments

Gauntlet Run #206

JOAN ELLIOTT PICKART

is the author of over sixty-five novels. When she isn't
writing, she enjoys watching football, knitting, read-
ing, gardening and attending craft shows on the town
square. Joan has three daughters and a fantastic little
grandson. Her three dogs and one cat allow her to live
with them in a cozy cottage in a charming, small town
in the high pine country of Arizona.

Dear Reader,

When I was first published as Robin Elliott with Silhouette Desire back in June of 1985, I was delighted to become a member of the Silhouette family.

Through the years, Silhouette Desire has become a favorite of readers across the country and around the world, a fact that doesn't surprise me. The Silhouette family has grown, and I have the privilege to be surrounded by very talented writers.

What *does* surprise me is how quickly the years have passed since that first Robin Elliott book was published. I feel as though I've traveled forward in time just as Dakota does in *Apache Dream Bride*.

To be chosen to be a part of the celebration of the 1000th Silhouette Desire novel is a tremendous honor. I salute the authors, who have contributed to the success of the Desire line, the editors, who have been those authors' partners, and I salute all of you who have been steadfast readers of our books through the years. You, too, are members of the Silhouette family.

While I began my Silhouette career as Robin Elliott, I am now writing under my own name of Joan Elliott Pickart.

Many thanks to all of you for your loyalty and support .

With warmest regards,

Joan Elliott Pickart

One

The June day was so perfect, Kathy Maxwell decided, it was as though Mother Nature had reached an agreement with the Prescott Chamber of Commerce to present the small northern Arizona town at its very best.

Kathy took a deep breath of the clean, cool air, and marveled yet again at how clear the bright blue sky was at an altitude of five thousand feet. The lack of smog and exhaust fumes was just one of a multitude of reasons that made her extremely glad she'd moved to Prescott from Chicago a year ago.

"Hi, Kathy," a woman called from across the street. "Are you playing hooky this afternoon?"

Kathy laughed. "You caught me, Beth. Sally is covering the store. I'm going to the craft show on the plaza with Lily."

"Enjoy yourselves," Beth said, waving as she went into a shop.

The people here were always so friendly and warm, Kathy thought as she smiled.

She had spent several summers in Prescott with her cousin, Lily, and had loved every minute of the visits. During her last trip west, she'd found herself consumed with an ever-growing sense of dread when envisioning a return to her life in Chicago.

The violence at the inner-city school where she taught increased each year, making it necessary to spend more time attempting to maintain order in the classroom than teaching the belligerent students.

During the previous school year, she'd lost weight, developed what were diagnosed as stress headaches and had difficulty sleeping. Admitting that she was burned-out had been difficult and had given her a feeling of failure. So, she'd hightailed it to Prescott, certain that a relaxing summer with Lily in the peaceful little town would render her as good as new. But by the end of August she realized it was not to be.

Not a risk-taker, and preferring order in her life, it had taken every ounce of courage Kathy possessed to quit her teaching job just weeks before the fall term began. Gathering that courage, as well as her savings, she had made a permanent move to Prescott and opened her store, The Herb Hogan. Her longtime hobby of growing herbs and studying their various uses had provided her the means to start her own business, which was thriving.

"Kathy, I'm coming, I'm coming," a voice said, bringing Kathy from her thoughts.

She turned to see Lily waddling toward her, moving as fast as anyone who was eight months pregnant could. Her cousin was short, and very round at the moment.

She had carrot red hair and a generous supply of freckles.

"Whew," Lily said, stopping next to Kathy. "I'll be so glad when this baby isn't getting free rides anymore. I swear he weighs more than the other three did, despite what the doctor says."

"You didn't have to rush. We have all afternoon to ourselves."

"What a heavenly thought," Lily said as they started down the sidewalk. "Brad was making lunch for the girls when I left the house. Oh, mercy, I don't even want to think about what my kitchen will look like when I get home. Brad is wonderful with the kids, but he's a disaster on cleanup detail." She paused. "So, tell all. How did your date with Roy go?"

Kathy wrinkled her nose. "Ask me anything you ever wanted to know about rodeos. I had a four-hour dissertation on the subject."

"Oh, dear, another dud. That's not good, not good at all."

"Lily, I'm going to say this . . . again. I've lost count of how many times we've discussed the subject. Are you listening?"

"No."

"Yes, you are. I'm happy in Prescott, very contented. Granted, there are adjustments to make when moving here from a large city like Chicago, but I've settled in quite nicely over the past year. This town is as close to perfection as a place can be.

"However, because it's so small, there isn't an abundance of eligible men. I've accepted that fact, and I'm aware that there's a very good chance that I'll never marry and have children. I'll spoil your kids rotten and be their eccentric spinster aunt. I'd rather live here alone than in Chicago where there were *beaucoup* men. And that, Lily Benson, is that."

"It certainly is not," Lily said with an indignant sniff. "There's a man for you in this town...somewhere. It's simply a matter of staying alert. Prescott is growing, you know. There are people moving here all the time.

"I made Brad promise to tell me if any bachelors retain him as their attorney. You've got to work on your attitude, Kathy, or you're liable to miss seeing a real hunk of stuff when he's right in front of your nose."

"Lily..."

"And," she went on, "let us not forget your many attributes, my dear. You're tall, disgustingly slender, have naturally curly blond hair, gorgeous blue eyes, and not one freckle, because I have your share. You're twenty-seven, intelligent, have your own business, adore children.... The list goes on and on. You're a super catch, Kathy Maxwell, and a fantastic man is going to come out of the ether and realize that."

Kathy rolled her eyes heavenward but kept silent, knowing it was useless to argue the subject further with her lovable and stubborn cousin.

The plaza, also called the square, was located on the main street and was a block long on each of its four sides. A majestic courthouse sat in the center, surrounded by trees and lush green grass. A charming gazebo had been built on one section of the lawn. Ongoing activities took place on the plaza, Kathy's favorites being the craft shows.

Handmade items were on display in the seemingly endless number of booths edging the grass of the square. Some of the people manning the booths were local citizens, others had come from across the country.

Kathy was slowly collecting items with Southwestern, as well as native American, themes to decorate her tiny cottage, which she adored. The one-bedroom house had a white picket fence, a tall juniper tree on one side, and a large backyard, where she grew herbs. Her home was "cozy and cute," she often told Lily, and it suited her needs perfectly.

"My stars," Lily said, "would you look at all the people on the square? What a crowd. See? I told you that Prescott is growing, and there's the evidence of it. Well, let's plough in and ogle the goodies."

"Did it ever occur to you that a majority of those folks are tourists?"

"Hush. Don't be negative. Mark my words, they live here."

"Yes, ma'am," Kathy said, laughing. "Anything you say, ma'am."

Late that night Kathy stood next to her double bed, a hammer in one hand. She cocked her head to one side, then the other, finally nodding in approval. She was delighted with the purchase she'd made at the craft show, and now it was properly placed on the wall just above her pillow.

"A Dream Catcher," she said, smiling. "I love it."

The native American creation was comprised of a three-inch circle covered in soft pink felt. Minute, taut webbing crisscrossed the interior of the circle, leaving a small hole in the center. Several felt streamers, six and eight inches long and decorated with beads and feathers, hung from the circle.

The legend of the Dream Catcher was enchanting, Kathy mused. Hung above where a person slept, the ornament would catch dreams that floated through the night air. Only good dreams would be allowed to pass through the hole in the center, while bad dreams were snared in the webbing and would perish at dawn's light.

"Pleasant dreams guaranteed," she said with a decisive nod.

She put the hammer away, locked the doors, then went to bed. She looked at the Dream Catcher once more before turning off the small lamp on the nightstand. With a sigh of contentment, she snuggled into a comfortable position.

What a lovely day it had been, she thought. As more and more time passed, she was emotionally reassured that she'd made the right decision when moving to Prescott. Her life was once again in order and her health restored. Everything was fine.

Except...

Kathy sighed. If she was totally honest with herself, she'd have to admit that she often yearned to have a special man to share with, to laugh and talk with; someone she loved and who loved her in return.

She wished to marry, have children, and still continue to nurture her growing business. She wanted it all, fairytale perfect, greedy person that she was. But the man, his love and the subsequent babies were missing.

She was learning to accept that fact. She refused to allow that empty place in her life to diminish her happiness and the sense of *rightness* about the choice she'd made to leave Chicago.

Who knows, she thought sleepily, maybe her Prince Charming *was* out there somewhere. He'd suddenly appear in her life and fall madly in love with her as he captured her heart.

Maybe...maybe...

Kathy drifted off to sleep.

* * *

She was standing in a field of glorious wildflowers, the vibrantly colored, fragrant blossoms dancing in the breeze as far as the eye could see. Her simple dress of pale yellow cotton fell to the tops of her bare feet. A sunbonnet covered her hair, tied loosely beneath her chin.

She was comfortable in the clothes, knew they were hers and were the proper attire for the West in 1877.

Raising one hand to shield her eyes against the brilliant sun, she stared into the distance with a sense of wondrous anticipation and excitement.

He was coming. Yes, she could see him now, racing toward her on his gleaming horse. Closer and closer he came, becoming clearer with every rapid beat of her heart.

Bronzed and beautiful, he rode bareback, clad only in buckskin pants and moccasins. His broad, tawny, muscled chest was glistening, his shoulder-length hair shining like ebony. His eyes were as dark as a raven's wing, and his features were bold, rough-hewn, with high cheekbones that were further evidence of his Indian heritage.

This was her love, her magnificent brave; proud, strong, riding like the wind, and coming to her, only her. He pulled the horse to a stop and dropped to the ground, striding toward her with sensual grace.

She opened her arms to receive him into her embrace.

"Hurry," she whispered. "Oh, please hurry, my love."

He was one step away, reaching for her, desire radiating from the depths of his obsidian eyes.

Then...

* * *

Kathy jolted upward in bed, her heart pounding. She heard the insistent shrill of the alarm clock and smacked it off.

"Blast," she said aloud. "I missed the best part of my wonderful dream."

She looked over her shoulder, intent on glaring at the Dream Catcher for not poking the dream through the hole earlier so it wouldn't have been cut short by the rude ringing of the alarm.

But the Dream Catcher wasn't there.

"Darn it," Kathy said, tossing back the blankets and leaving the bed.

She was certain she'd secured it firmly with a nail tucked through the loop at the top. Apparently, though, both nail and Dream Catcher had fallen to the floor during the night.

"That's strange," she said, seeing the nail still in the wall.

Kathy dropped to her knees and peered under the bed, discovering only a few dust bunnies. Rising, she slid her hand between the mattress and the wall. Nothing.

Where on earth had the Dream Catcher disappeared to?

"Coffee," she mumbled, starting toward the door. "Coffee, then a more thorough search."

She yawned just as she reached the foot of the bed, then stopped, statue-still. Her mouth remained opened from the now-forgotten yawn and her eyes widened. A strange squeak escaped from her throat, and she snapped her mouth closed. The sound of her frantically beating heart echoed in her ears.

The missing Dream Catcher was on the floor between the bed and the wall.

But it was no longer three inches around. It was six feet across!

And there, caught half in and half out of the center hole, lying on the carpet with his eyes closed, was the Indian brave from her dream!

Her trembling legs refused to hold her for another instant, and Kathy sank onto the edge of the bed, her horrified gaze riveted on the enormous Dream Catcher and the man caught in the webbing. He hadn't moved. The steady rise and fall of his chest were the only indication that he was even alive.

No, Kathy thought frantically, he *wasn't* alive. Well, he wasn't dead, either. But he was most definitely not alive in the sense that he was actually there in her bedroom. That was ridiculous. Impossible. Absurd.

Kathy jumped to her feet, stomped back to the head of the bed, then yanked her Mickey Mouse T-shirt straight over her bikini panties. After getting into bed, she pulled the blankets up to her chin and squeezed her eyes tightly closed.

That Indian, she told herself, that absolutely gorgeous-beyond-belief man, was *not* in her bedroom because she was still asleep and dreaming. It was one of the most wide-awake-seeming dreams she'd ever had, but it was a dream, nonetheless. The alarm would go off at any moment now and she'd begin her daily routine on a perfectly normal Monday morning. Fine.

Several minutes passed as Kathy stayed ramrod stiff under the covers. Then she very tentatively opened one eye to sneak a peek at the clock.

"Oh, dear heaven," she said, with a near-sob.

It was long past time for the alarm to ring *because it had already rung!*

She was awake. *She was honest-to-goodness awake.* The empty nail on the wall above her head seemed to scream at her that the pretty little three-inch Dream Catcher was no longer *there,* because it was now six feet around and holding fast to the most magnificent man she had ever seen.

Kathy Maxwell, she admonished herself, stop it. Just cut it out. This was *not* really happening, because things like this *didn't* really happen. There was a perfectly reasonable explanation for this nonsense, but, oh, mercy, she wished she knew what it was.

She eased herself slowly upward, hardly breathing, then crawled on her hands and knees toward the end of the bed.

There was, Kathy told herself, nothing on that floor but a section of brown carpet that needed vacuuming.

As she came to the foot of the bed, she closed her eyes, causing her to nearly fall off the end.

Slowly, very slowly, she opened her eyes. At that exact same moment, the Indian opened *his* eyes and looked directly at her.

"Aaak!" Kathy screamed.

She scrambled off the side of the bed and came to a stop at the man's feet. He turned his head to stare at her, a frown knitting his dark brows.

"Oh. No. Oh, dear," Kathy said in a voice that was more of a whimper. She hopped from one foot to the other, wringing her hands. "No, no, no."

"A death dance?" the Indian said. "I'm dead. So be it."

Kathy stopped in mid-hop, and leaned slightly forward. "My goodness, you have a marvelous voice. It's so deep and rich. Well, that figures. You're a big man and your voice is exactly right for your size. I suppose your tan is natural, what with your being a native American and... No! I'm not talking to you. I refuse to say another word, because you're not really here. Are you getting this, mister?''

"I'm dead," he said, then sighed. "I thought I had lived my life with honor befitting a Chiricahua Apache, but apparently I have angered the gods. I have been sentenced to spend my eternal beyond with a shrieking witch-woman."

Kathy planted her hands on her hips and narrowed her eyes. "That was very rude. I am *not* a shrieking witch-woman, for Pete's sake. How would you feel if your Dream Catcher grew from three inches to six feet and plopped a guy from *your* dream on the floor in your bedroom? Huh? Answer that one. You'd be shook up, too."

"Dream Catcher?" he repeated, glancing at the apparatus surrounding him. "Yes, this is a Dream Catcher, but I have never seen one this large. Why am I being held captive in this enormous Dream Catcher?"

"Beats me," Kathy said, shrugging. She giggled, realizing at once that there was a hysterical edge to the sound. She pressed one hand to her forehead. "No fever. Drat. But, darn it, this is *not* happening. It just can't be."

The Indian began to shift, struggling to escape from the tight webbing surrounding the center circle where he was held fast.

"Don't you move," Kathy said. "I'm warning you, I'll call the police, and the sheriff, and the fire department, and... and... I mean it, you stay right there."

The Indian glowered at her and continued to wrestle with the Dream Catcher. Kathy inched backward until she thudded against the wall, then wrapped her hands around her elbows in a protective gesture.

She watched with wide eyes as the man worked his way free.

One part of her exhausted brain was terrified at the thought of what he might do to her.

Another section of her frazzled mind was mesmerized by the intriguingly sensuous and blatantly masculine play of the bunching muscles beneath his taut, tawny skin.

Yet another piece of her mind continued to deny that this bizarre scenario was taking place.

"Mmm," the Indian said as he accomplished his goal. He rolled to his feet in a smooth, graceful motion, standing close to six feet tall.

"Don't kill me," Kathy said, her voice trembling. "Don't scalp me. Don't do anything, except go away." She flapped her hands at him. "Shoo. Be gone. Disappear. Right now."

"Woman," he said gruffly, crossing his arms over his broad chest, "you talk too much. I must be dead. There's no other explanation for this. Unless..." He narrowed his eyes. "It is possible, although I seriously doubt it, that you possess magical powers that you combined with those of the Dream Catcher. Indian legends and folklore should not be tampered with. Not ever."

Kathy shook her head. "I don't have any magical abilities. And I certainly didn't tamper with the powers of the Dream Catcher." She paused. "I hung the Dream Catcher above my bed, deciding its legend was enchanting. Then just before I fell asleep I was thinking about how wonderful it would be if a special man... I had a dream about... Oh, dear heaven. No, forget it. This whole thing is impossible."

"I agree. Therefore, I am definitely dead."

"No," she said, sighing, "you're not dead. I can't explain this. I don't really believe it, but... I wish you'd crawl back into that Dream Catcher and transport yourself to 1877 where you belong."

"If I am not dead, if I am actually here, I would prefer not to be. But I do not possess the power to command a Dream Catcher." He shook his head. "No, I refuse to believe this is happening."

Kathy inched her way carefully around him to sink onto the edge of the bed.

"Look," she said, "we agree that this really isn't taking place, but repeating over and over that it can't be true isn't getting us anywhere. Let's just stop for a minute and take the approach that it *did* happen. That's probably very foolish, but I'm getting a tad desperate here."

The Indian shrugged. "It *is* foolish, but I do not have a better idea right now."

"Fine. We'll just calm down and discuss this like mature adults. I suppose I should introduce myself. I'm Kathy Maxwell. Do you have a name?"

"Dakota."

"Dakota what?"

"Dakota what?" he repeated, obviously confused.

"Don't you have a last name? Two names?"

"One man. One name."

"Oh, well, that's reasonable, I guess, considering the fact that no one in your tribe would be putting together a telephone book."

"Pardon me?"

"Never mind. Dakota, this is not 1877. It's 125 years later than that, give or take a handful."

"That is ridiculous."

"I know, but for now we're pretending that it isn't ridiculous. Okay? Do you remember what you were doing before you woke up here?"

He nodded. "I was riding my horse on open land. There were wildflowers in all directions. My thoughts were—" He stopped speaking and frowned. "An Indian brave deals with his own problems, solves them privately."

"Dakota, please," Kathy said gently, "I understand and respect that, I truly do, because I often keep troubling things within myself, too. But this is so important. Share with me, tell me what you were thinking as you rode through the wildflowers. Your inner feelings are safe with me, Dakota."

He stared at her for a long moment, and she met his gaze directly, aware that he was weighing and measuring, deciding if he would do as she'd asked.

"Yes, all right," he said with a weary-sounding sigh. "I was dwelling on the condition of my life, the emptiness of it, the loneliness. My people have all gone to the reservation, but I chose not to go, not to be penned up like an animal. I could not survive like that, and I knew I had to stay behind. Yet at that moment, I was wishing I had a place to belong, somewhere I could call home."

"Oh, Dakota," Kathy said, hearing the pain in his voice, "I'm so sorry."

He cleared his throat. "My thoughts were interrupted as I saw a woman standing in the distance. A white woman. I did not know her, but then...I *did* know her. I was going to her, she was waiting for me. This does not make sense, because I would never approach a white woman."

Kathy got to her feet. "Yes, it *does* make sense, because that was my dream. Oh, my gosh, Dakota, don't you see what this means? I somehow connected to your airwaves, or brain waves, or something. That was *me* standing there in that yellow dress. Do you understand?"

"Then you *did* tamper with the powers of the Dream Catcher."

"Not intentionally. I bought it at a craft show because I thought it was pretty and I liked the legend it represented. Dakota, I hate to say this, but I think we'd better start accepting the fact that you really were transported through time in the Dream Catcher."

"I do not know, I just do not know. How is it that you speak Apache?"

"I don't. I'm speaking English and so are you."

"No. I know only my native tongue."

Kathy threw up her hands. "This is more evidence that this whole thing is true. We're both talking in our own language, but we can understand each other. That must be part of the Dream Catcher's power."

"I will have to think about this," Dakota said, shaking his head. "I speak so you can understand me in this era, yet I wear my own clothing." His gaze slid over the soft T-shirt Kathy wore. It clearly outlined the swell of her breasts. "Is that your usual attire? Is that an image of the god you worship?"

For the first time since the bizarre beginning of the morning, Kathy became acutely aware of her scanty attire. The Indian's dark eyes seemed to be peering through her shirt, scrutinizing her bare breasts beneath.

She could feel the heat from his penetrating gaze. It touched a place deep and low within her, churning, swirling, causing a flush to stain her cheeks. She was pinned in place, unable to move, having to remind herself to breathe.

This man, she thought hazily, was real. He was there. Denying his existence was foolhardy. There was no lingering doubt in her mind that he had been flung through time and space to arrive in the present from the past.

She had somehow managed to dream about a living, human being, rather than a creation of her imagination. The potent powers of the Dream Catcher had then captured him and brought him to her.

But why?

The magnitude of what had taken place was too enormous, too overwhelming, to be chalked up to some weird cosmic glitch.

Why had this happened to her and Dakota?

"Kathy?"

"What? Oh, my clothes. I don't go outside like this. I wear this to sleep in, that's all."

"And that image? Is that who you worship?"

"Heavens no," she said. "That's Mickey. He's not a god, he's a mouse." She paused. "Dakota, the only way that I can deal with all of this is to accept the facts as they stand and give it all a semblance of reality, even if it's not reasonable reality. Oh, dear, I'm not making sense. What I'm saying is, until I have just cause to change my mind, I'm going to believe you were transported from 1877 to now through the Dream Catcher."

"You have the right to do what you wish."

"And you? What do *you* believe is happening here?"

Dakota sighed. "I do not want to believe it. There's no purpose to my being here. Yes, I was feeling lonely, alone, but there's no life for me here in the future, in the white man's world. I do not belong here, Kathy.''

"We don't know that, Dakota. If we accept this scenario as being the truth, as being what actually happened, then we have to move on to the question of *why* it occurred.''

"The why is because you tampered with the powers of the Dream Catcher. The question is not why, it is how. How do we send me back to my own time? I don't want to be here, Kathy, and I have no intention of staying.''

"Dakota,'' she said quietly, "maybe there is something important that you're supposed to do here. Yes, all right, to be fair to you we should be trying to figure out how to send you back. But I truly believe we should also be considering the question of why you are here, what it all means.''

"Mmm,'' he said, frowning.

"Will you think about both issues? Please, Dakota?''

He stared at her for a long moment before answering.

"Yes,'' he said finally, "I will think about both. That will enable me to postpone, at least for a while, the bleak thought that we may never know the answer to either of those questions. We may *never* know.''

TWO

Why?

The question beat against Kathy in time with the water from the shower.

Perhaps she was placing too much emphasis on that question, adding to the situation further complexity that didn't need to be there.

It could very well be that it was all a fluke, an unexplainable event that had been created by the powers of the Dream Catcher. There was no mysterious, hidden meaning and purpose to discover. It had simply happened.

The magic of the Dream Catcher had interwoven with the thoughts she'd had just before falling asleep of wishing for a special man in her life. She'd dwelled on what was missing from her life, rather than counting the blessings that she had. Her musings had created the dream of seeing Dakota in the field of wildflowers.

Back in time Dakota had been thinking similar thoughts, acknowledging his loneliness, yearning for a place to belong, a home that was once again his.

Like a silken thread from a tapestry, the Dream Catcher had woven through her dream and onto Dakota's thoughts, pulling them together, uniting them.

But why?

Oh, darn it, Kathy thought as she dried herself with a fluffy towel. She couldn't seem to move past believing that there was an important and definite reason for what had happened.

She stopped for a moment and stared at the bathroom door.

What if she'd imagined the whole thing? She'd return to her bedroom, the pretty little Dream Catcher would be hanging on the wall and there would be no Dakota, because he didn't exist.

What was more terrifying? That Dakota was really there, or that he wasn't, meaning she was slowly but surely losing her mind?

"Fine, Kathy," she muttered, "ask yourself some more questions to boggle your brain."

Dakota. If he was real, truly there, she was going to have to be very, very careful. For that one brief moment he'd had an unsettling effect on her. Man to woman. Like nothing she'd ever experienced before.

That was not going to happen again.

Dakota stood in Kathy's bedroom, his eyes darting around. He felt claustrophobic in the small space and had to draw on inner strengths to keep from finding the way to the outdoors as quickly as possible. Even the windows were covered in some sort of hard, clear substance that he could see through, but which sealed the room further.

He moved to the end of the bed to stare at the giant Dream Catcher where it lay on the floor, a frown on his face.

The powers of a Dream Catcher were well known and respected by his people. He had, indeed, been carried far into the future to a place like none he'd seen before and was held captive there.

He dragged both hands down his face, then shook his head.

No, he didn't want to believe that, because he did *not* want to be here. This was the white man's world that offered him nothing but danger and a lack of acceptance. He would be feared and, therefore, hated.

Dakota laughed, the sound harsh and short, having a bitter ring to it.

It was no different for him in his own time. He faced danger at every turn from the soldiers who sought him. Indians of all tribes were feared and, thus, hated for the color of their skin and the way they chose to live their lives.

He had told Kathy Maxwell that he wanted to go back to where he belonged. Belonged? He belonged nowhere, as everything he had possessed had been taken away and was no longer his to have.

The white people were greedy and cruel. They'd claimed the Apache land for their own, sending the Indians to reservations like penned animals.

But he hadn't gone. Not Dakota. For many, many moons now, he'd been alone, roaming the land, hiding whenever he saw soldiers riding near. He'd not spoken to another living being in a very long time.

Until Kathy.

She was the first white woman he'd seen up close, and he'd been startled by the blue of her eyes. It was as though the gods had given her pieces of sky to see with. Pretty eyes. Eyes like the sky, hair like the sun. *Very* pretty. She would give a man fine sons.

Kathy.

Her name was moving easier through his mind now; and did not seem quite so strange. When he first beheld her, looked at all of who she was, which was the custom of his people, he had felt the shaft of heat streak within his body to coil low and tight. He'd wanted to join with her, man and woman.

That thought *must* be ignored. The matter of importance was to find a way to have the Dream Catcher send him back to where he'd come from. It was lonely and empty there, but at least he knew it for what it was.

Dakota narrowed his eyes as he stared at the Dream Catcher, willing it to speak to his mind, give him the answers he needed.

But the Dream Catcher was silent.

His attention was drawn to the carpet, and he hunkered down, running one hand over it.

How did Kathy grow soft, brown grass in her house? What manner of soil had she packed hard for her floor to have produced this crop of vegetation?

He placed his hands on his thighs and pushed himself upward to stand staring at the Dream Catcher again.

"Dakota?"

He spun around at the sound of his name being spoken in a quiet voice.

He saw Kathy in the doorway, wearing a red shirt of some sort, and man-pants of dark blue. She'd painted her mouth with light red, and her short, sun-colored hair was damp, curling over her head and brushing her pale cheeks.

The heat of desire rocketed through him again. Was she casting a spell over him, causing him to lose control of his basic needs, the command of himself, that he took great pride in?

"Are you all right?" Kathy asked.

"Yes, I'm all right."

"While I was dressing I thought perhaps I'd imagined—" she swept one arm through the air "—all of this, you, the huge Dream Catcher. But what has happened to us is true. You *are* here, Dakota, and we have no choice but to deal with that fact."

"Mmm."

Kathy sighed. "I'm exhausted. The day has hardly begun and I'm so tired. This has been a very draining experience. I... Oh, my gosh, I have to get to work. I'm going to be late opening the store."

She started from the bedroom, then halted her step, turning to face him again.

"I can't leave you alone all day," she said. "There are too many things here that would be new to you and you might hurt yourself. Besides, we need to concentrate on finding a solution to this... this mess. I'll call Sally and ask her to cover the store."

She hurried into the living room and telephoned Sally, who cheerfully agreed to run The Herb Hogan.

"I'll be fine tomorrow," Kathy said. "I don't feel well because... because my allergies are bothering me."

"I didn't know you had allergy problems," Sally said.

"I didn't, either. Life is full of little surprises," Kathy said. And six-feet-tall surprises, too.

"We have herbs for helping allergies, Kathy."

"Oh, yes, of course. Silly me. I forgot. I'll probably come into the store later and fix myself up as good as new. Thanks for covering on short notice. Bye."

As Kathy replaced the receiver she turned to see Dakota standing in the doorway.

"Where is your man?" he said.

Kathy blinked. "My man? I don't have one."

"He died?"

"No, I've never been married. In this time era, women often live alone."

"Then who protects you? Feeds you? Makes a home for you?"

"*I* do," she said, splaying one hand on her chest. "I take care of myself."

"That's not the natural order of men and women. Women do not have the skills or strength to do men's work. Wearing man-pants won't help you achieve what you are not capable of doing."

"Man-pants? Oh, you mean my jeans. It's appropriate for women to wear...well, man-pants. These," she went on, lifting one foot, "are tennis shoes. They come in all colors. I have on white ones, but I own a blue pair, a red pair, a... Never mind. I have a feeling you don't give a hoot about tennis shoes."

Dakota shrugged.

"You're positive you feel all right?" Kathy said. "It occurs to me that it might be very hard on a person to be hurled through time."

"I'm fine, except for being hungry."

"You need some food? Well, all right. Maybe if we do something ordinary like having breakfast we'll be able to approach this whole thing more calmly. Yes, that's a good idea. When in doubt...eat."

In the kitchen, Kathy immediately decided that if she attempted to explain to Dakota what a stove, refrigerator and microwave were, they'd never get around to eating. For now, she'd just let him be totally confused about all the paraphernalia.

She opened the refrigerator and removed bacon, a carton of eggs and a quart of milk. A few minutes later, the bacon was sizzling in a frying pan as she wire-whipped eggs and milk in a bowl.

Out of the corner of her eye, she saw Dakota tentatively touching things, sometimes leaning forward for a closer look, before moving on to the next item that beckoned.

This kitchen, Kathy thought, was too small. Well, that wasn't exactly true. It wasn't big enough when she was sharing it with Dakota. There was more than just his size causing her to feel suddenly crowded and unsettled, it was also the aura of masculinity emanating from him. His raw, earthy, male essence was sensuously overwhelming.

She was acutely aware of her own femininity to the point that her skin tingled. Dakota was man. She was woman. Those facts should be nothing more than simple data. But it *wasn't* simple for some mysterious reason.

No, she'd covered that topic while she was getting dressed. She was not going to fall prey to Dakota's male magnetism. He wasn't a man, he was a problem to be solved.

With a sigh, Kathy forked the bacon onto a pad of paper towels, drained the majority of the grease into a coffee can at the back of the stove, then poured the frothy egg mixture into the pan. Staring off into space she stirred the eggs in a steady rhythm with a slotted spoon.

A problem? Oh, dear, that was putting it mildly. She wished she could decide that this whole scenario couldn't possibly have taken place and, therefore, it hadn't. But she'd run out of ways to attempt to convince herself that it wasn't true. Dakota was most definitely there.

"Smoke," Dakota said, from where he stood behind her.

"What?" Kathy said. "Oh, my gosh, I've burned the eggs."

She quickly lifted the frying pan to another burner on the stove, muttering under her breath as she vigorously stirred the eggs.

"Woman," Dakota said, "you don't cook well. I think perhaps you've spent too much time trying to do men's work and have neglected learning how to properly perform your duties."

"That's great, just dandy," she said, glaring at him. "I have a 1877 chauvinist on my hands. So, okay, this meal is a disaster, but I'm not my usual organized self this morning. This *is not* the way I ordinarily start my day. Got that? And don't call me 'woman'."

"You *are* a woman."

"I realize that, but the way you say it is demeaning. My name is Kathy." She paused. "Oh, Dakota, I'm sorry. I didn't mean to be so cross with you. I'm upset by all that's happened. Let's take a deep breath and eat breakfast, such as it is."

She carried the meal to the table. Dakota followed her and stared at a chair. He watched Kathy settle onto one, then splayed a hand on the seat, pressing down on the smooth wood to determine its strength.

"It will hold your weight," Kathy said. "Trust me."

Dakota eased himself onto the chair, his muscles tensed should he find it necessary to move away quickly. A few minutes later he relaxed and scrutinized the offering on his plate.

The bacon was crisp, but the eggs were burned in spots and runny in others. He looked at Kathy, and watched in fascination as she shoveled eggs onto a fork.

"What is that tool?" he said.

"This? It's a fork." She poked it into her mouth, pulled it back out empty of eggs, then chewed and swallowed. "See? It's a way of getting the food where it needs to go. Try it."

He wrapped one large hand around the fork handle, jammed the prongs into the eggs, then jerked his hand upward, spilling the contents.

"Slowly, Dakota, gently. Try it again."

"Mmm," he said, glaring at her.

Kathy smiled as she watched him attempt to master the strange tool called a fork. He moved cautiously this time, and she could see him assessing the challenge with intelligence and determination. Yet, there was also an endearing, little-boy quality to the scene that caused a warm, fuzzy feeling to tiptoe around her heart.

"You did it," she said, clapping her hands as Dakota chewed a delivered forkful of eggs.

He swallowed, then frowned. "This tastes terrible."

Kathy shrugged. "If you don't like it, don't eat it. It's up to you."

"I need the nourishment. Bad cooking is better than nothing, I suppose."

"Don't push me, Dakota."

"Push you?" he said, looking directly into her eyes. "I would never harm you, Kathy. I am an Apache. I re-

-spect women, I respect you. I wouldn't push you, beat you or strike out at you."

"Oh, I didn't mean . . ."

"If you have your nose split someday, it would be by your choice."

"Pardon me?"

"An Apache woman who commits adultery has her nose split so everyone will know what she has done, that she was not true to her man."

"That's gross. Just eat the awful eggs."

They finished the meal in silence, each lost in their own thoughts.

"Dakota," Kathy finally said, "do you have any knowledge, understanding at all, of how to get the Dream Catcher to reverse what it did?"

"No."

"Great," she said with a sigh. "What if I have to actually dream about sending you back to where you belong? That would be impossible. A person can't dictate to their subconscious like that." She paused. "What if we both sat on the floor by the Dream Catcher and concentrated on the same message? You know, kept mentally repeating 'Send Dakota back to 1877.'"

Dakota shrugged.

"Do you want to try it?"

"The idea has merit," he said, nodding. "I must heed nature's call first." He got to his feet.

"Wait," she said, jumping up. "I have to explain about bathrooms and . . . This is so bizarre. Oh, well, come on. I've got a nifty little room to show you."

Two hours later, Kathy flopped back onto the living room carpet and closed her eyes.

"I'm exhausted," she said. "Brain dead. I can't concentrate anymore. We've been sitting on the floor forever next to this giant menace, and it's not working."

"No, it's not," Dakota said. "This plan is not the answer."

Kathy got to her feet, then slouched onto the sofa. "Now what?"

"I don't know."

"Dakota, are there people worried about your disappearance. I mean, do you have a family? A...a wife? You said that you were riding alone through the wildflowers but..."

"I don't have a wife. I have no one now," he said quietly. "My people have gone to the white man's reservation. I refused to go. I have been alone for many moons."

Kathy straightened to look directly at him. "I'm sorry. You're from 1877. Yes, I'm remembering my history. The Indians in this area were moved to reservations around 1875. Someone who wouldn't go was called a Bronco Apache, meaning one who is alone, no longer a part of a tribe." She paused. "I can only imagine what it has been like for you, Dakota. The image in my mind is so stark and empty. An existence of such chilling loneliness."

Dakota stared at the Dream Catcher, but didn't reply.

"Maybe I'm wrong," she said. "I'm viewing it from how I'd feel. You were having thoughts about loneliness, but on the whole you may have been perfectly happy living like that. You might not need other people."

"My body can survive if I am alone, but my spirit suffers. A man who is truly a man is complete enough within himself to have room for others. There's an emptiness in solitude that goes on for too long. I have needs, Kathy. I have needs."

He turned his head slowly to meet her gaze.

I have needs, Kathy.

His words echoed in her ears and a reply was whispered again and again from her heart. *I have needs, too, Dakota.*

Dakota nodded slowly, and Kathy registered a flash of panic, suddenly wondering if he could read her mind. If not, then what blatant message of desire was radiating from her eyes and visible on her face?

She felt stripped bare, vulnerable, with no defenses against the potent masculinity of this man.

I have needs, Kathy.

And wants? she thought. Was he as aware of her as a woman as she was of him as a man? Or did he see her as nothing more than an annoying product of the powers of the Dream Catcher?

Oh, Kathy, stop it, she admonished herself. What Dakota did, or did not, think of her was not important. Her reactions to him as a man meant nothing, would not be allowed to mean anything. No.

She had concentrated as hard as she could as they'd sat by the Dream Catcher, sending their mutual message that Dakota be transported back to 1877. She'd tried her best.

Or had she? she now wondered.

Had she held something back from the focus of her thoughts? Had the tiny portion of her heart that didn't want him to leave...not yet, please, not yet...been more powerful than the truth of what must be done?

Oh, she didn't know. She was confused, tired, excited, frightened, all in one jumbled maze.

She had *so many* questions with no answers.

Three

___

Dakota suddenly rolled to his feet, startling Kathy back to attention.

"The Dream Catcher," he said, "must be kept in a safe place. I don't want to stay here, in this world, and if anything happens to the Dream Catcher, I'll have no hope of returning to my own time."

"We can slide it under my bed," Kathy said, pushing herself off the sofa.

"Fine."

Kathy stopped and looked directly at him. "I realize that this whole scenario is overwhelming. Your traveling through time, and encountering all the new and strange things that you've never seen before, must be very unsettling. Even so, I can't help but wonder if you've considered staying here."

"No."

"Dakota, what would you be going back to, other than loneliness and danger? Do you really want to spend the rest of your life on the run, hiding from the soldiers, never able to settle in one place?"

He splayed one hand on his chest. "*I* didn't choose the way of my existence, it was the white man's doing. The choice I *did* make was not to go to the reservation with my people. I'm prepared to live with the consequences of that decision."

"But you don't have to, don't you see? You'd be accepted here, judged only by who you are as a man, not by your heritage. Oh, Dakota, you've said yourself that the Dream Catcher has great powers. Couldn't it be possible that you were *meant* to be here for some reason?"

"Such as? Do your people need to be taught how to live off the land, fish and hunt for their food, build shelters to live in?"

"Well, no, but..."

Dakota shook his head. "Then the Dream Catcher has no purpose for my being here."

"You don't know that to be true."

"Kathy, there's no point in discussing this any further. I intend to do everything possible to enable me to go back to 1877."

"But..."

"That is enough! Let's put the Dream Catcher under the bed."

Kathy sighed, then they carried the Dream Catcher into the bedroom and carefully maneuvered it beneath the bed.

Back in the living room, Dakota folded his arms across his chest and frowned as he looked at Kathy.

"There's something disturbing me that I cannot put to rest," he said. "Why are you alone? Is there something about you that doesn't please the men of this time? I beheld you, which is Apache custom. I have seen you on the outer side and sensed who you are within. You please *me*, Kathy Maxwell. I would give serious thought to making you my woman."

"I..." Kathy started to reply, then snapped her mouth closed as she realized she had no idea what to say.

A strange warmth swept through her as Dakota's words echoed in her mind. What he had said was one of the most exciting, yet frightening, things she had ever heard. *Dakota's woman.*

Oh, stop. She wasn't going to dwell on it a second longer. Dakota was simply curious about the customs and social structure of this era.

You please me, Kathy Maxwell.

Kathy, she scolded herself, just cut it out right this second.

"Well, you see, Dakota," she said, wishing her voice was steadier, "choosing a life's partner is much more complicated now. It's done more slowly, carefully. I have to be as pleased, as you put it, with the man as he is with me. Just looking at someone, beholding them, isn't enough."

"Why not?"

"Because there are discoveries to be made first."

"Such as?"

"Well, values. You know, your stand on truth, trust, fidelity. Then there's stuff like what do we have in common? How do you spend your leisure time? How do you feel about security, a home, children, a woman who has her own business and wouldn't give it up for the world?

Then there's . . . Oh, good night, you aren't really interested in all of this, are you?''

He nodded. "It fascinates me. You've listed what people in this time must discover about each other, and most of it is reasonable." He paused. "No man has pleased you as you made these discoveries?"

Kathy shrugged. "No. Emotions come into play here, too, you know. There has to be love that is real and rich and deep. But, no, I haven't found the man I want to spend my life with."

"*I* please you."

Kathy blinked. "I beg your pardon?"

"You beheld me. I can tell from what I've seen in your eyes that you desire me. You have had thoughts of joining with me, man to woman."

A flush of embarrassment heated Kathy's cheeks. "Well...um...you're a very handsome, well-built man, Dakota. I'm a healthy, normal woman who... Oh, for Pete's sake, this is ridiculous."

"No, it isn't," he said, shaking his head. "I did not ask to come here and I do not intend to remain. However, while I'm here I wish to understand this world. To learn and enrich my mind. A man who isn't constantly attempting to add to his knowledge is lazy, worthless. You have customs that are new to me, things you can teach me during my stay."

"But what if when you go back you don't even remember having been here?"

"So be it. It's important that I live for the moment I am in. That's the Apache way. Each beat of our heart is to be cherished.

"Apaches also pride ourselves on our patience. If we encounter an enemy who outnumbers us and it would mean certain death to engage them in battle, we withdraw to fight another day when we will be assured of a victory. That isn't cowardly, it is wise. We place high value on life, living. We don't treat lightly the gift of the body we were given to walk the earth in."

"That's a lovely philosophy," she said quietly. "People in this time era could use some of that kind of common sense."

"I haven't betrayed the Apache way," Dakota went on, "but I've had to struggle to maintain my patience. My people were robbed of their land, their way of life. They were herded like animals to the reservation, never again to be free. Patience will change nothing."

"I'm so sorry about what was done to the Indians back then. I've only read about it, but I realize you're suffering the pain of it right now."

"I've been alone these many moons," he said, his voice gritty, "and questions with no answers have plagued me. Now I've been brought here where I don't wish to be, but at least I can ask questions and have them answered. I can learn.

"I am a man, Kathy, a proud Apache brave. All I wanted was a place, a home, a sense of self and worth. I wanted a woman of my heart and sons of my seed. The white man hasn't killed my body. *I won't let them crush my spirit.*"

Tears filled Kathy's eyes as she heard the raw emotion in Dakota's voice, saw it on his face and in the depth of his expressive dark eyes. Before she'd realized she had moved, she had wrapped her arms tightly around his waist and rested her head on his chest.

"No one is going to crush your spirit," she said, tears echoing in her voice. "We won't let them, Dakota. *We won't*. I'll teach you whatever you want to know about this era, if that's what you want, if that will make you feel better about being here."

Dakota encircled Kathy with his arms, then buried his face in the soft tumble of her curls, savoring the fragrance of flowers.

"We haven't solved the mystery of the Dream Catcher's powers," he said. "We don't yet understand the Dream Catcher's spirit call to enable us to send me back. So while I'm here we will live for the moment we hold in our hands."

Dakota's words echoed in Kathy's mind as she stayed nestled against his warm, massive body. He felt wonderful, smelled wonderful. Being held in his strong arms was wonderful. Desire was beginning to churn hot and low within her.

But there was more than basic physical yearnings involved. Dakota was touching an emotional place deep within her that she hadn't even known existed. She was beginning to feel connected, bonded to him. She had *felt* his pain as he'd spoken of what had been done to his people. The chill of his loneliness as he'd roamed the land alone was an icy fist within *her*.

While I am here, we will live for the moment we hold in our hands.

Did she have the courage to actually do that? Could she live for the moment, treasure what they might share, then be prepared to let him go? How long would she ache for him when he was gone? How long would she cry?

Oh, she couldn't think straight. Too much was happening so quickly that she was off kilter and terribly confused. She was going to put her emotional turmoil on hold, she had to.

Dakota inhaled Kathy's feminine aroma once more, then moved her gently away from him.

"What discovery do you want to make first?" he said.

Kathy laughed in spite of herself. "You make this sound like research for a term paper."

"A what?"

"Never mind. I'm such a wreck that a dose of practical thinking is called for. Therefore, we'll shift our focus. You need some clothes."

"I have clothes."

"Yes, but you don't have a shirt. Men in this era are free to go without a shirt, but not all of the time. You need a shirt."

He shrugged.

"So, I'm going shopping and buy you a shirt. I'll get you some jeans, too. Man-pants. Do you shave?"

"What?"

"Do you grow hair on your face that you cut off each day?"

"No," he said slowly. "Kathy, are you talking nonsense?"

"No. White men grow hair on their faces. I've read that most Indians don't, and I guess it's true. Okay. Cancel the shaving cream and razor. Do you—" she paused, feeling the now-familiar warm flush creep onto her cheeks "—use underwear?"

"I don't know the meaning of that word."

Dandy. Go for it, Kathy. "Do you have anything on beneath your pants?"

Dakota frowned. "For what purpose? Do white men wear pants under their pants?"

"Well, yes."

"Strange. No, I don't have this underwear you speak of."

"Good. I've never bought Jockey shorts in my life. Dakota, listen to me. You must promise that you'll stay inside the house while I'm gone. You can't go wandering around until I think of a way to explain who you are and why you're here."

"I need to breathe fresh air. The walls are closing in on me."

"Oh, dear. Well, all right. Let's go into the backyard and have a stroll. I'll show you my herb garden. Then will you be able to stay inside while I go shopping?"

"Shopping is what you do to get me a shirt?"

"Bingo. I mean, yes, that's correct."

He nodded. "I'll agree to your plan. We'll see your herb garden now."

They left the living room, went through the kitchen, then Kathy stopped on the enclosed sun porch beyond.

"This is where I dry my herbs," she said, sweeping one arm in the air.

Dakota looked at the multitude of plants covering the walls of the sun porch. Kathy had designed, then hired a handyman to build, the drying walls with pegs where she hung the herbs, utilizing every spare inch of space.

"I can't grow everything I need for the store," she said, "but I'm pleased with what I'm able to add to the inventory myself. I get most of my teas from a woman in Sedona, and the oils and lotions from Flagstaff. I also sell commercial vitamins.

"I dry the herbs here, then put them in brown paper bags because they must be kept in a dark, dry place. I take the bags to The Herb Hogan. That's the name of my store."

"It's good," Dakota said, nodding. "You've tended to your herbs as it should be done. No Apache woman could do better."

"Oh, well," she said, smiling, "thank you. That was a very nice compliment."

She was pleased to the point of ridiculous by what Dakota had said. It shouldn't matter what he thought of her talents, but the warm, fuzzy feeling she was registering was evidence that it did. She was as adept as an Apache woman would be at growing and caring for herbs? Goodness, wasn't that something?

Dakota continued to scrutinize the herbs, then finally nodded again.

"Are you ready to go outside?" Kathy said.

Dakota started toward the door, then stopped, looking through the window.

"No. It's too open, with nowhere to conceal myself if the soldiers come."

"Dakota, there aren't any soldiers trying to find you to take you to the reservation. Your people are free now. Free. They can go anywhere they want to. They live, work, play, right beside white men if they choose. Some are still on Indian land, on reservations, but it's because they want to be, not because they're forced to stay there. You have nothing to fear by leaving the shelter and safety of this house."

He looked at her for a long moment. "I'll trust what you say, Kathy. These are peaceful times?"

"Not everywhere, I'm afraid, but here in Prescott it's peaceful."

"Mmm," he said, then followed her out the back door.

It was another picture-perfect day. The air was clean, the sky a brilliant blue with a sprinkling of fluffy white clouds.

Dakota spread his arms wide, closing his eyes as he inhaled deeply, then slowly exhaled. Opening his eyes again, he swept his gaze over the multitude of neat rows of Kathy's herb garden.

"This is good," he said, nodding. "The soil is rich here?"

"Yes, it's excellent. I have it tested to be certain it's in proper balance. This year I added some iron."

"Mmm," he said, walking forward.

Kathy watched as Dakota started along the first row of the garden. He stopped often, hunkering down to gently grasp a leaf between his thumb and forefinger, then rose again and went on.

He moved with such a smooth flow of motion, she mused, like a graceful animal in the wilds. He was comfortable in his own body, his command and control over it a given.

Kathy had dated several men in Chicago who worked out regularly at health clubs. But now, looking back, she realized they wore their bodies like merit badges to be recognized and fawned over.

But there was more than just the "realness" of Dakota's physique that was giving her food for thought. His openness and honesty when he talked to her was also far different from what she'd known.

Dakota spoke from his heart, holding nothing back. He'd shared his pain and loneliness with no concern for an image of machismo. He wasn't caught up in modern-day posturing, the real-men-don't-eat-quiche syndrome.

He was so real, so rare, so special.

Dakota, Dakota, she thought. *What are you doing to me?* No, she wouldn't dwell on Dakota, the man himself. She mustn't allow herself to do that because it was dangerous and foolish. He didn't even want to be here.

He was sort of "on loan" from the past until they could master the mysteries of the Dream Catcher.

Great, she thought dryly, now she was making him sound like a library book she needed to return. But in a way, that was true. He had to go back to 1877, where he belonged.

"Feverfew," Dakota said, bringing Kathy from her tangled thoughts. "It has a bitter taste, but eases head pain."

"Yes, it works wonders for headaches and migraines. A few drops of peppermint in the drink helps the flavor. Of course, peppermint is worthwhile on its own. It aids digestion, reduces nausea and vomiting, and is often soothing to peptic ulcers." She laughed. "I sound like a commercial on television."

Dakota frowned.

"Oh, my, you don't know about television. I don't watch it much, because I'd rather read a good book. I enjoy football games during the season, but... I'm confusing you terribly, Dakota. I'm sorry."

"There's a great deal to learn about this time you live in."

"That's true," she said quietly, "but I'm beginning to think you have things to teach me, too. People now seem so caught up in their possessions and appearances. What they have is often more important to them than who they are. *Really* are."

Their eyes met as he walked slowly toward her, finally stopping directly in front of her.

"Are we making discoveries?" he said.

"Yes, Dakota," she said, smiling, "we're making discoveries."

"Good. Well, I've breathed the fresh air and escaped from the walls that were closing in on me. I'm renewed.

I'll stay inside while you go shopping for the shirt you say I must have.''

"I'll go right now," Kathy said, "and get back here as quickly as I can."

After Kathy left the house, Dakota sat on the floor in front of the box she had described as being a television. He glanced at the picture that showed people moving and talking, but didn't really see it, his thoughts turned inward.

A part of him, he knew, was angry that he had been transported from his world to this one. Wasn't it enough that the white man had been controlling his existence, without the powers of the Dream Catcher taking hold of his destiny, as well?

What purpose could possibly be served by his being here in this time? None. Yes, he could learn, enrich his mind with knowledge he hadn't had before, but as far as he could tell it wouldn't be useful information once he returned to 1877.

Kathy was convinced there was a definite reason for what had taken place, a meaning, a message, that they didn't yet understand. Was she right? He didn't think so.

Kathy. Kathy Maxwell.

The concept she'd outlined of a man and woman making discoveries about each other was interesting. He fully intended to explore that theory further, to discover more about Kathy.

She pleased him. She made his blood run hot, his manhood ache to join with her womanly body. He liked the color of her eyes and hair, her aroma, the way she fit so perfectly against him when he'd held her in his arms.

A sudden chill swept through Dakota, pulling him from his thoughts, and causing him to stiffen as a wave of dizziness followed the cold. He drew a rough breath, then shook his head to clear away the dark mist that had begun to dim his senses.

What was wrong with him? He'd never felt such a strange sensation. Was he ill? He was a strong, healthy brave who was rarely sick. Whatever it had been that had assaulted him was gone, leaving no reason to dwell further on it.

Dakota shifted his attention to the television and concentrated on what there was to see in the box.

Less than an hour later, Kathy drove toward Lily's house with the fervent wish that her cousin would be at home.

Kathy had bought Dakota two western shirts with pearl snaps. One was royal blue, which she thought would look wonderful with his bronzed skin. The other was black and gray in a typical western-shirt pattern of stripes and plaid. She'd also purchased two pairs of jeans, which she hoped would fit him. She had not, thank goodness, had to buy him any underwear.

As she approached Lily's house, she rehearsed an explanation as to who Dakota was and how he'd come to be in her home.

After three attempts, she mentally threw up her hands in defeat. No matter what she said, she was going to sound like a loony tune. What if Lily refused to believe her, decided Kathy had slipped over the edge and hauled her off for professional help?

So, don't tell her, Kathy argued in her mind. No, that was dumb. She and Lily saw each other often, were in and out of each other's homes. Lily would *definitely* notice that a tall, dark and handsome Apache had taken up residence in Kathy's cottage.

Besides, she needed Lily and Brad's input and suggestions as to how it might be possible to send Dakota back to his own time.

Don't start, Kathy Maxwell, she told herself. She had to ignore how thoroughly depressing the thought of Dakota's leaving was becoming. The fact remained that he had to go, because he didn't belong here. Even more, he didn't *want* to be here.

But...

"Kathy, shut up," she said aloud as she pulled into Lily's driveway.

Her cousin had the inner door opened and the screen locked. Kathy rang the bell, and two little girls instantly made a beeline to answer the summons.

"Hi, Aunt Kathy," one of them said.

"Hi, sweetheart. Can you unlock the door?"

"No, Mommy says I have to get her if someone comes. Bye." She turned and ran across the room.

"But it's me, your Aunt Kathy," she called after her. "Oh, well. How are you, Holly?" she said to the other child.

"Two," the toddler said, holding up that many fingers.

"No, not how *old* are you, just how are you? Never mind, Holly. You're two, and that's great. I wish I was two, and didn't have any problems except refusing to be potty trained."

"Two. Two. Two," Holly said.

"Kathy," Lily said, lumbering toward the door. "What's wrong? Why aren't you at The Herb Hogan?" She unlocked the screen door and pushed it open. "Come in, come in. What's going on?"

Kathy entered the large living room decorated in attractive but very sturdy furniture meant to withstand the wear and tear of an active family. A generous supply of toys cluttered the carpeted floor.

"I took the day off because—" Kathy paused "—because I took the day off. Oh, dear."

"Sit," Lily said, pointing to the sofa. Kathy slouched onto it. "Girls, play with your toys so I can talk to Aunt Kathy."

"Cindy is in school," the older girl said, "'cause she's six. When I'm five, I can go to school, but I'm four. I want to be five, Aunt Kathy."

Kathy smiled. "You'll be five next year, Mary Kathy. The time will pass very fast, you'll see."

"Mary Kathy," Lily said, "take Holly into the family room, please. You're building a castle out of blocks, remember?"

"And I'm the princess of the castle, Holly," Mary Kathy said, taking her sister by the hand. "You can't be the princess 'cause I am."

"Two. Two. Two," Holly said merrily, allowing Mary Kathy to lead her from the room.

"Now, then," Lily said, sitting down in a chair and automatically resting her hands on her protruding stomach. "Speak."

"Yes, well, I... Well, um... Lily, I... Oh, dear heaven."

"Good grief, Kathy, what is your problem?" Lily said, frowning. "I've never seen you so befuddled. What on earth is the matter?"

Kathy sat up straighter on the sofa, cleared her throat and lifted her chin.

"Okay, here goes," she said. "When we were at the craft show yesterday I bought that pretty little Dream Catcher, as I'm sure you recall. I was intrigued by it, and not only was it lovely, but the legend was so enchanting. So! I hung the Dream Catcher above my bed to do its thing. You know, only let nice dreams through the hole in the center, and snag the nasty dreams in the webbing. That's how it works, you see. Well, I went to sleep..."

"Kathy," Lily yelled, "take a breath."

Kathy jumped at Lily's sudden outburst.

"My stars," Lily said, "you're talking a hundred miles an hour. You have to be about drained of oxygen. You'll scare the bejeebers out of the girls if you pass out on the floor."

"Oh. Sorry. I'm a tad shook up." Kathy took a deep breath and let it out slowly. "There. I'm fine." She pressed one hand on her forehead. "No, I'm not. I'm a wreck, a total wreck."

Lily leaned as far forward as her stomach would allow. "Why? What wrecked you?"

"Dakota."

"Who?"

"Oh, Lily, you've got to believe me. I had a dream about a gorgeous...I'm talking magnificent here... Indian brave, who was riding across acres of beautiful wildflowers to come to me. Me! Goodness, I wonder if Dakota is worried about his horse. The poor animal must be terribly confused. One minute Dakota was there, then...poof...he was gone. Would a horse notice something like that?"

"Kathy!"

"Oh. Yes, well, there I was, dreaming my nifty dream. The Indian was walking toward me, ready to take me into his arms...and the alarm clock went off."

"Damn."

"That's what I said. At first. But then. Oh, dear heaven, Lily. Dakota...that's the Indian's name...was on my bedroom floor! The Dream Catcher had grown to about six feet across, and he was caught in the hole in the center. It's true, I swear it. He's at my house right now. I explained what a television was, told him the people weren't really in that little box. I *think* he understood.

"Anyway, I left him watching TV so I could go shopping for him, buy shirts and jeans. He doesn't use underwear. I cooked him breakfast, which was a culinary disaster, but he said I grow herbs as well as an Apache woman, which pleased me to no end. We tried to send him back through the Dream Catcher, but it didn't work. I need your help, and Brad's, too. Okay?"

Lily sank back in her chair and stared at Kathy with wide eyes. She opened her mouth to speak, shook her head and closed her mouth again.

"You don't believe me," Kathy said, her shoulders slumping. "I can tell by the look on your face."

"I'm mulling this over," Lily said.

"Mull faster."

"Kathy, a couple of years ago my friend, Elsie, was very unhappy. She'd just gone through a messy divorce, she had no idea what to do with her life, she felt useless, with her self-esteem at rock bottom."

"And?" Kathy prompted.

"I convinced her to go to a craft show on the square with me to get her mind off her problems for a bit. There was a native American selling strings of Spirit Bells in one of the booths. They're colored beads and bells attached to cords. Each color of bead is supposed to bring you different rewards when you hang the Spirit Bells in your house. Red is for love, yellow is prosperity, green is for plentiful crops, and on the list goes.

"Well, Elsie was really taken with the whole idea. Blue is for peace and tranquillity. That's what she yéarned for, inner peace, instead of the emotional turmoil she was in. So, she asked the Indian if he would make her a small string with bells and only blue beads. We strolled by the rest of the booths, then went back to get Elsie's custom-made Spirit Bells."

"What happened?" Kathy said, now sitting on the edge of the sofa cushion.

"From the moment that Elsie hung the Spirit Bells in her house, things began to change. Out of nowhere it seemed, she began to come up with solid plans for her future. She enrolled at Yavapai College, saying she had a long-buried dream to become a teacher.

"She polished her typing skills so she could work as a secretary while going to school. She sold her house and moved into a cute condo that wouldn't overwhelm her with upkeep. She found her inner peace. To this day, she believes it's because of those blue beads. And I believe it, too."

"Oh, my," Kathy whispered.

"Kathy Maxwell," Lily said firmly, "I do hereby declare there is a gorgeous Indian in your house who was transported from the past through your Dream Catcher. His name is Dakota, and he doesn't use underwear."

"Oh, thank you, Lily, thank you."

"What on earth are you going to do with him?"

While he's here, Kathy thought, we'll live for the moment we hold in our hands.

"Kathy?"

"Who? Oh. What am I going to do with him? During the time he's here he wants to learn about this era, and he's teaching me about his people, his beliefs. We're...we're sharing, discovering.

"He doesn't want to stay here, Lily. He sees no purpose for his being here, yet I find myself more and more convinced that there's a definite reason this happened.

"Oh, I don't know. It's all so confusing, so hard to comprehend. At first I refused to believe he was real and had actually traveled through time. But it's true. He's really here."

"Amazing," Lily said. "But I believe it, too. Indian powers are very strong, Kathy. You must have some kind of power yourself to have been able to connect with Dakota through the Dream Catcher. Goodness, this is really something."

"I know," Kathy said, getting to her feet. "I've got to get home because I don't want to leave Dakota alone too long. There are so many things for him to explore that he's never seen before. I'm afraid he might injure himself."

"Good thought." Lily pushed herself to her feet with less-than-graceful form.

"Lily," Kathy said, "could you get a sitter on such short notice so you and Brad could come to my house tonight? Four minds working on a dilemma are better than two."

"Brad is in Phoenix for a dinner meeting. We could come tomorrow night, though."

"All right. Thank you." Kathy frowned. "Attorneys are very logical people. Is Brad going to believe this story?"

Lily laughed. "No problem. He handled Elsie's divorce and knew what condition she was in mentally and emotionally. My husband, the logical attorney, now has Spirit Bells hanging in his office, with every colored bead that has a purpose. He said he was going for the whole nine yards. After this baby is born, I intend to inform him he's to remove the purple beads from those cords.''

"What is purple for?''

"Passion.''

Kathy laughed. "Oh.''

"I don't want Brad to turn into an ice cube, you understand, but four kids is enough.'' She lowered her voice to a whisper. "This one,'' she went on, patting her stomach, "was conceived in Brad's office. I walked in and... Well, the purple beads go, or I'm never visiting him at his office again. We'll be over tomorrow night, Kathy. Brad will definitely want to meet Dakota. So will I, for that matter. Gorgeous?''

"Incredible.''

"Very interesting.''

"Thank you so much, Lily,'' Kathy said, giving her as much of a hug as was possible. "I'll see you tomorrow night.''

"Two. Two. Two,'' Holly shouted, toddling into the room.

As Kathy drove away from Lily's, a sense of anticipation began to blossom within her.

She was going home.

She was going home to Dakota.

Four

Kathy entered the house through the front door and dropped her packages and purse on the nearest chair. Dakota was sitting cross-legged on the floor in front of the television and did not acknowledge her arrival.

That was an appropriate position for an Indian, Kathy thought, smiling. Oh, goodness, she was glad to see him. She'd never "come home" to anyone before, and it felt so right. No, it was more complex than that. It felt right because it was Dakota.

"I'm back," she said cheerfully. "Did you enjoy yourself while I was gone?"

"Mmm," Dakota said, still staring at the television screen.

Kathy crossed the room to stand behind him, curious as to what program he was watching that held his undivided attention.

"A soap opera?" she said. "Oh, heavens, Dakota, people don't really have that many crises in their lives. Well, maybe some do, I suppose, but not the average person. On the soaps, everyone is shown to extreme. You know, the nice people are very, very nice, and the crumb-bums are very, very crummy. I'm not sure that soaps are the appropriate thing for you to watch because you'll get a distorted impression of..."

Kathy stopped speaking and blinked in surprise as Dakota suddenly rolled to his feet and turned to face her. He gripped her upper arms, pulled her close and covered her mouth with his.

Kathy's eyes flew open in shock, but in the next instant her lashes drifted down and her arms encircled Dakota's waist. She slipped her tongue between his slightly parted lips to seek and find his tongue, feeling him tense for a moment at her bold intrusion.

The kiss deepened and heat thrummed within Kathy, deep and low. Hot. So very hot. It began to pulse in a maddening, tantalizing tempo that matched the beat of her racing heart.

She slid her hands upward, splaying them on his bare back, savoring the warmth of his skin and the feel of the taut muscles beneath her palms.

Dakota dropped his hands and wrapped his arms around her, nestling her to his body. Her breasts were crushed against the solid wall of his chest, creating exquisite images in Kathy's mind of Dakota soothing the sweet pain with his hands and mouth.

She could feel his arousal pressing against her, hard and heavy, and her passion soared even more. A hum of pure womanly pleasure whispered from her throat.

She was on fire, Kathy mused hazily. Going up in flames.

This kiss, this incredible kiss, was like nothing she'd experienced before. Her senses were heightened. The feel, the taste, the aroma, of Dakota were magnified. She was acutely aware of every inch of her own body, as well, rejoicing in her femininity.

Dakota, her heart and mind sang.

He broke the kiss and released her so abruptly that she staggered for a moment. They each drew a ragged breath, then their gazes met, desire radiating in eyes of sky blue and eyes of ebony.

"That," Dakota said, his voice raspy, "was definitely a discovery."

"It certainly was," she said, a rather wistful tone to her voice.

"What is this called, this joining of mouths we just shared?"

The last of the sensual mist encasing Kathy dissipated. "A kiss. We were kissing. What do the Apaches call it?"

"We don't . . . kiss."

Kathy's eyes widened. "You've never kissed anyone before?"

"No. I saw it done by the people in the box, the television. It seemed to give them pleasure. One man spoke of wanting his woman after they'd kissed and she agreed, said she wanted him, too. I assumed this was part of the ritual that takes place before men and women join their bodies. I wanted to discover what it felt like to share it with you. This kissing is, indeed, pleasurable." He nodded. "Yes, I like it."

Kathy moved around him and turned off the television. "I think you've seen enough for one day. I must say, Dakota, that for someone who has never kissed anyone before, you did a sensational job of it."

"It pleased you?"

"Oh, my, yes."

"Good. Then I'll kiss you again," he said, reaching for her.

"No," she said, taking a step backward. She thudded against the television. "I don't think that would be a terrific idea."

"Why not? You said it pleased you."

"It did, but it made me feel... That is, I wanted to... Well..." Her voice trailed off, and a warm flush stained her cheeks.

"Mmm," he said, appearing extremely proud of himself. "You wanted to join with me. That's good, very good. Kissing was an excellent discovery. We're moving closer to the time of joining."

"No, we're not," she said, her voice rising. "Yes, okay, I want you, I want to join with you. It's called making love, if the proper emotions are involved. But it isn't going to happen between us, Dakota."

"Why not?"

She folded her arms over her breasts. "Listen to me carefully. I do *not* take the act of joining, making love, lightly."

"Nor do I."

"Fine. Then you should be able to understand that it's too risky. What if I... Darn it, what if I fall in love with you and then you zoom back to 1877? What then, Dakota? I would miss you. I would cry. I have to protect myself from that kind of heartbreak."

"I would miss you, too, Kathy," he said quietly. "My heart would be heavy, sad."

Kathy nodded. "Then you understand why we mustn't kiss anymore, and why we're not going to make love, join. This discussion is over."

"For now."

Kathy sighed, shook her head, then hurried to the chair where she'd placed the packages.

"Try on your new clothes," she said. "That's safe enough."

She turned to see Dakota inching down his buckskin pants.

"Wait a minute," she said. "Stop that."

"How can I try on new clothes if I don't remove my old clothes?" he said.

"You can't take off your clothes in the middle of the living room, for Pete's sake. You do it in private, alone, behind a closed door."

Dakota frowned, digesting what she'd said, then shook his head.

"No, that's wrong," he said, his voice low. "We're supposed to be on a journey of discovery. We've discovered a great deal already, Kathy. One of those things is that kiss. Another is that we want to join, make love, but you have fears to put to rest first."

"Dakota..."

"Hear me," he said, raising one hand. "I agree with the reasons for this journey of discovery, and I feel there's no shame in your viewing my body naked, in its natural state. Don't you see, understand the importance of the discoveries we would make if you stood naked before me, and I before you? It's the way it should be."

She was dying, Kathy thought frantically. She was dissolving. Her bones were melting. Dakota's voice seemed to be caressing her like rich velvet, the sensual words fanning the embers of desire within her into leaping flames once more.

But there was even more involved than just the sexual aspect of what he was saying. There was also the simplistic honesty that was so real and pure that he was introducing to her world from another era.

When, how, in the decades since Dakota's time, had everything changed, become so complex? The honesty was now buried beneath games played between men and women, beneath the struggle for equality, then on to the battle for power and control.

Dear heaven, she thought, what a precious gift Dakota was giving her by just being himself. It was as though he was sweeping away the cobwebs so she could see, *really* see, the truths of her world.

What she had always accepted, she now questioned. The way it was, was not necessarily as it should be.

She needed to take an inventory of herself, discover not only things about Dakota, but rediscover herself, as well.

She'd been awakened from complacency.

She would never be the same again.

She would never want to be.

Because of Dakota.

"Kathy?" he said, bringing her from her reverie.

"Dakota, I heard what you said, I listened. I need to think it all through, because what's very simple to you is terribly complex for me.

"Please be patient with me while I'm attempting to unravel the maze in my mind. Would you please go into the other room to remove your clothes?"

Dakota looked directly into her eyes, then nodded slowly. He gathered the packages and left the room.

"Oh-h-h, my," Kathy said, sinking onto the chair. "Who are you, Kathy Maxwell? What do you want?"

She sighed, leaned back in the chair, forced herself to blank her mind and waited for Dakota.

When he reentered the living room, Kathy's breath caught as she stared at him. She got slowly to her feet, her gaze sweeping over him.

"You look..." she started, then swallowed. "Wonderful."

The jeans appeared as though they'd been custom-tailored just for him. They hugged his narrow hips and muscled thighs with delicious perfection.

He'd chosen to wear the royal blue shirt, which did, indeed, do fantastic things for his bronzed skin and marvelous physique. His shoulder-length black hair shone like polished ebony as the sunlight pouring through the window cascaded over him.

"Do you like those clothes?" she said.

"Mmm. The pants are stiff, not soft like my own, but they're acceptable."

"New jeans are always stiff. Why don't you go put your own pants back on, and I'll wash the jeans. That will soften them a bit."

"Do you still want me to be naked where you can't see me, or was once enough?"

"Go," she said, laughing, flapping her hands at him. "No, wait," she added, in the next instant. "You should see how great you look. I have a full-length mirror hanging behind my bedroom door."

"To see how I look as a man of *this* time?"

"Well, yes, you *look* like you belong here. You could walk around downtown with me and no one would be the wiser. But, oh, Dakota, you aren't like us, the people of this era. You're special and rare, like a treasure that should be cherished. You're what man once was, but has forgotten how to be. Don't change. Oh, God, Dakota, don't change."

"What are you talking about?" he said, frowning.

"Never mind," she said, waving one hand in the air. "I know I'm not making sense but... Come on, let's go into the bedroom."

In the bedroom, Kathy closed the door to reveal the mirror.

"Okay, step over here by me," she said.

Dakota moved to stand beside her, and they both looked at the mirror.

"Oh, merciful saints," Kathy whispered.

She grasped Dakota's arm, her eyes widening in horror as she continued to stare at the mirror.

Dakota wasn't there.

The mirror reflected only her, her hand in the air, holding nothing.

"Dakota?" she said, a ring of panic in her voice. "What does this mean? What's happening? Why can't we see you in the mirror?"

"Now I understand why I felt so strange before. I thought for a moment that I was ill," he said, a muscle jumping along his tightened jaw. "I was transported to your time through the Dream Catcher. My body is here. But, Kathy, my spirit stayed in the place... in the place where I belong... and must return to."

Kathy's heart raced as she looked into the mirror again, then back at Dakota.

"Your spirit, your soul," she said, her voice trembling, "was separated from you? It remained in 1877? Why?"

Dakota took a step backward. "I don't know, Kathy. My head pains me and I need some solitude, some peace. The walls are closing in on me again. I'm going outside to the garden."

Kathy watched him as he strode from the room, then she stared at the mirror, wrapping her hands around her elbows as a chill swept through her.

How terrifying it had been to see only her own reflection when she *knew* Dakota was standing beside her. She felt as though a part of *her,* as well, had been torn from her, ripped away.

Why had this happened to Dakota?

Was it due to the magical powers of the Dream Catcher being tampered with, instead of respectfully left alone?

Or had Dakota, himself, been subconsciously struggling against the forces hurling him forward in time?

What had he meant when he said he'd felt strange, thought he was ill?

More questions. More questions without answers.

Kathy massaged her temples with her fingertips.

Now *she* was getting a headache. She and Dakota needed a break from all of this. As soon as he returned from the herb garden, she'd suggest they go for a relaxing drive, beyond the city where Dakota wouldn't have to see anyone.

Yes, that was a good idea. They'd seek solace in the peacefulness of nature, pretend they were the only two people in the entire world.

Five

Deciding that she and Dakota would have a picnic supper, Kathy retrieved a white wicker hamper from the front closet shelf and set it on the kitchen counter.

As she prepared sandwiches, she moved often to where she could see through the sun porch window to the yard beyond. Dakota had settled onto a small patch of grass, sitting Indian-style and staring into space. His back was ramrod straight, and his hands were fanned on his knees.

He'd withdrawn and was turned inward after the startling episode with the mirror, Kathy mused. And so had she. They were each lost in their own thoughts.

As Kathy sliced pickles, she sighed. Then she sighed again, becoming aware of how often she was producing the sad sound.

Darn it, she scolded herself, *cut it out.* She *knew* Dakota had to return to his own time in history. That fact had been a given from the very beginning of this bizarre experience.

But the incident with the mirror had spelled things out in painful reality, leaving nowhere to hide from the stark truth.

Dakota could *not* stay here.

With her.

"Oh, damn," she said, then sniffled.

She was acting so ridiculous, it was disgusting. She'd only known Dakota for a handful of hours. He'd arrived unexpectedly, he'd leave as soon as the mystery of the Dream Catcher was solved, and that would be that.

"Fine," she said, then reached for a bag of potato chips. "No, it is *not* fine."

As she continued to pack the hamper, she gave herself a stern lecture on not behaving like an adolescent. She told herself to accept things as they were, to get her act together instantly.

"Forget it," she mumbled. "I'm not listening to one word I'm saying."

She was Kathy Maxwell, but she was not remotely close to being the same Kathy Maxwell who had hung the pretty little Dream Catcher above her bed and gone blissfully to sleep. She was changed.

It was difficult to explain even to herself, but, somehow, in the few short hours they'd been together, Dakota had become an important, intricate part of her life.

He had looked at her and really *seen* her. He had beheld her and knew who she truly was. For him, all she had to do was *be,* and it was glorious.

Oh, Lord, she was miserable, she thought, filling a thermos with lemonade. The image in her mind of Dakota disappearing back through the hole in the center of the giant Dream Catcher was devastating. She would miss him so much, so very much.

Kathy closed the lid on the hamper just as Dakota entered the kitchen. She took a steadying breath and turned to look at him, forcing a lightness to her voice when she spoke.

"I thought it would be nice to get out of the house for a while," she said. "We can drive beyond the city to a quiet place and have a picnic."

"Picnic?"

She patted the hamper. "Supper."

Dakota nodded.

A short time later the hamper and a blanket were on the back seat of Kathy's blue compact car. Dakota stood next to the passenger door, his arms folded tightly over his chest, a deep frown on his face.

"Dakota," Kathy said, "*please* get in the car."

"No."

"It's perfectly safe," she said, flinging out her arms. "I drove it when I went shopping for your clothes, and I came back all in one piece. Remember? This automobile is an example of the type of transportation we use now. It's a modern-day horse." She paused. "Or whatever."

"Mmm."

He glared at her, then walked slowly around the car, peering at the tires, looking in the windows, rapping his knuckles on the hood.

"I don't like it," he said, shaking his head. "Why would anyone go willingly into a metal, egg-shaped box to be held captive while it moves on the road with other metal eggs? There's no sense in this, Kathy."

"You've got a point there," she said thoughtfully, then blinked. "No, you don't. Please, Dakota, trust me." She opened the passenger door. "Get in. Okay? It's comfortable, just like a chair."

After giving her one more dark glower, he moved tentatively onto the seat.

"You're a tad scrunched," she said, "because you have such long legs." She reached across him and clicked the seat belt into place. "There. Snug as a bug."

She closed the door, then ran around to the driver's side. After getting in and fastening her seat belt, she turned the key in the ignition. Dakota tensed even more as the engine roared.

"Stay calm," she said, shifting into reverse. "Here we go, nice and easy."

As she backed out of the driveway, then drove slowly, very slowly, away from the house, Dakota began to relax.

He did *not* like this metal egg, he reaffirmed in his mind, but there seemed to be no alternative but to sit there, tied in place like a captured coyote.

His instincts told him that Kathy should not be in this thing, either. She had no man to take care of her, keep her from harm. While he was there, *he* would protect her. *He* would be her man.

He was her man, his mind echoed. She was his woman. There was a bond between them, something special, like nothing he'd experienced before. He wanted to join with her to make love, yet it was more than that. He cared about Kathy. He wished to see only happiness in her eyes of sky blue and on her lovely face. Kathy Maxwell had become very, *very* important to him.

A chill swept through Dakota as he glanced at Kathy.

He now knew that he had no spirit, no center. It had not come with him when he'd been transported through the Dream Catcher. And it wasn't there to provide him with the ongoing flow of the essence of who he was.

He had to go back to his own time.

He had to leave Kathy.

And he knew, just somehow knew, that she would cry when he left her.

He turned his head to stare out the side window in a futile attempt to catalogue all the new and strange sights he was seeing.

Nothing really registered, as his mental vision was filled with images of his life in 1877. He saw himself alone, roaming the land, hiding from the soldiers. With the pictures, came the ache of loneliness.

He closed his eyes to draw courage and strength from deep within himself, to accept his fate with the quiet dignity befitting an Apache brave.

But thoughts tumbled through his mind in a confusing maze of contradictions. He didn't want to stay in this era, in the white man's world that was so difficult to understand. His own time was simple; man united with nature and lived in harmony with the land. Yet the thought of going back to the existence he'd had was bleak, dark and very empty.

Why? Why had all of this happened to him? Why had the Dream Catcher snared him and brought him here? Why had he been connected with Kathy by the magical powers? He didn't know the answers to any of his questions. He just didn't know.

Dakota blanked his mind by force of will, and directed his attention to the scenery beyond the window of the car.

* * *

For the picnic, Kathy selected a secluded area tucked beneath towering trees. It was high above the city, providing a breathtaking view for miles.

The only sounds were chattering squirrels, chirping birds and the rustle of leaves on the trees as an occasional breeze whispered through on its way to somewhere else.

Seated on the blanket, Kathy and Dakota consumed every bit of the delicious meal. They hardly spoke, each intent on relaxing, allowing the tension and stress within them to ebb.

When their appetites were satisfied and the debris placed in the hamper and set off to one side, they both took deep breaths and released the air at the same time, causing them to laugh in unison. The joyous sound seemed to echo through the crystal-clear air, cascading back over them tenfold.

"This was a good plan," Dakota said, smiling. "Thank you."

"You're welcome." Kathy paused. "You have a marvelous smile, Dakota. You should use it more often. Native Americans ... Indians ... are often thought of as being stoic, not revealing their emotions, but feel free to smile whenever the mood strikes."

He chuckled. "I'll remember that." He laid back on the blanket, lacing his hands beneath his head.

Kathy sat cross-legged next to him, sweeping her gaze over the glorious view.

"Strange," Dakota said.

"What is?" she said, turning her head to look down at him.

He freed one hand from under his head and extended it toward her.

"Come down here by me," he said. "I want to show you something."

Kathy hesitated for a moment, then did as he asked, stretching out next to him. There was just enough room between them for their entwined hands.

Was this a smart idea? Kathy asked herself. The heat emanating from Dakota's massive body seemed to weave over and through her, swirling and thrumming low within her. He was just so male, and just so there, and she was just so aware of every rugged inch of him.

"The sky," Dakota said quietly.

"Who? Oh. Yes, it's very blue, isn't it?"

What a brilliant thing to say, she thought, mentally rolling her eyes. She was going to shut up before she said something else as equally dumb.

"Yes," Dakota said, chuckling, "it's very blue."

Oh, good night, Kathy thought. That sexy sound of his was sinful. The heat within her was now pulsing, tightening in a spiraling coil.

Dakota's smiled faded. "Ever since I was a boy I'd steal moments like this to lie in a bed of grass and stare at the sky. It gave me a sense of peace. It always had a calming effect on me.

"No matter what was happening in my life, the sky was consistently there. It was something I could count on to steady me, like a rock. Does that make sense?"

"Yes," Kathy said softly. "Yes, it does."

"Your eyes remind me of the sky, Kathy. I've never seen eyes as beautiful as yours. Blue, so blue. Sometimes I gain an inner peace by looking into your eyes. Other times they cause me to burn with the want of you."

"Well, I..." Kathy started to say, then stopped speaking as she realized there wasn't a rational thought within her reach.

"Looking at the sky now," Dakota went on, "it struck me that it's the same as it is in my own time. That's what I meant when I said it was strange. I expected it to be different somehow, but it's not. It makes me feel...connected. Yes, that's the word. Connected."

"To 1877? To where you...belong?"

He released her hand and rolled up on his side, bracing himself on one forearm and looking directly into her eyes.

"No. It makes me feel connected to *your* time in history. To where I am now. Connected to you."

"Oh," she whispered, unable to tear her gaze from his mesmerizing dark eyes.

Dakota raised his hand and began to trace her features with the tip of his index finger. Kathy shivered from the tantalizing foray. Dakota's fingertip was callused, but his touch was so gentle. Her heartbeat quickened.

"I have never," he said, his voice raspy, "felt such soft skin as yours. Apache women spend hours each day in the sun, and their skin becomes dark and leathery at an early age. Your face is as pale as a new moon, and feels like the pussy willows that grow by a stream. Soft, so soft."

Then he slowly, so slowly, lowered his head to claim her mouth with his. His tongue slipped between her slightly parted lips to seek and find her tongue, stroking it sensuously with his own.

Kathy's arms floated upward to encircle his neck, her fingers weaving through the thick, silky depths of his hair. She urged his mouth harder onto hers.

She didn't think. Couldn't think. Didn't wish to think. She wanted only to feel, to give full rein to the passion and emotions flowing through her.

Dakota shifted on top of her without breaking the kiss, catching his weight on his forearms. Kathy could feel his arousal heavy against her, a promise of what he would bring to her as a man.

She savored the taste of his mouth, his aroma of fresh air, soap, and the musky scent of building desire. She heard the rumble of want escape from low in his chest, and rejoiced in the knowledge that he wanted her as she did him.

Her breasts ached to be caressed by his strong but gentle hands. Her femininity pulsed with heat, the flames licking through her. A whimper of need fluttered in her throat.

Dakota tore his mouth from hers to draw a rough breath.

"I want to join with you. To make love," he said, "here, beneath the blue sky, in nature's bed."

"You once said," Kathy said, hearing the thread of breathlessness in her voice, "that while you are here, we'll live for the moment we hold in our hands."

"Yes."

"I wondered if I could do that, if I had the courage, because I'm not a risk-taker. I will choose the safe road whenever I can. But, oh, Dakota, I do want you so much. I've changed since you came into my life. I *do* have the courage to live for the moment, *our* moment."

Dakota looked at her, simply looked at her. The intensity of his desire was there for her to see and believe in. Kathy trembled.

He shifted off of her, and with hands not quite steady, they removed their clothes.

Don't you see the importance of the discoveries we would make if you stood naked before me, and I before you? It's the way it should be.

And it was.

They discovered. They rejoiced in the beauty of each other, the perfection, the wondrous differences that made Kathy, woman, and Dakota, man. They burned with the want and need to mesh their bodies into one entity.

Dakota stretched out again next to Kathy, then kissed her deeply once more.

Discovery.

With hands and lips they journeyed, explored the mysteries the other's body revealed, then cherished each other as precious treasures. Tastes, textures, aromas, all mingled together. Desire built to a fever pitch.

"Dakota," Kathy whispered. "Please."

"It is time," he said quietly. "*Our* time. This is the joining of our marriage bed. From this moment, for the moment we hold in our hands, we are one."

He moved over her then, catching his weight again on his forearms.

"Kathy."

"I'm yours, Dakota."

He entered her body, the moist heat receiving him, welcoming him, all of him. For a long moment he was still, as they savored.

Then slowly at first the tempo began, the dance, the ritual as old as mankind, yet new and theirs alone.

Kathy matched Dakota's rhythm in exact synchronization, lifting her hips to meet him, clinging to the taut muscles of his arms.

Harder. Faster. Pounding in a cadence that stole their breath and caused their hearts to race.

It was ecstasy.

It was beyond description in its splendor, a union like nothing either had ever known. They no longer knew where their own body stopped and the other's began. They were truly one, joined.

The tension grew in tightening coils deep within them, swirling, churning. Creating a near-pain so exquisite it brought the name of the other to their lips in awe and wonder.

On and on. Discovering, discovering. Higher. Hotter.

Then . . .

"Oh, Dakota!"

Kathy was flung into glorious oblivion. Shattered into a million pieces, each as vibrantly colored as the wildflowers had been when she'd first seen Dakota. She called his name over and over, clinging to him with a grip far greater than her normal strength.

Seconds later he joined her there, as his life's force spilled from him into her, granting his release from passion's hold. He threw his head back with a roar of masculine pleasure. He, too, saw the multitude of colors, knew they were the wildflowers where Kathy had beckoned to him, and exalted in the knowledge.

They hovered there as the last rippling spasms swept through their bodies. Then they began to drift slowly down, into the welcoming sea of the fragrant, bright flowers, then further yet to come to a reality still encased in a hazy, sensual mist.

His strength spent, Dakota collapsed against Kathy, then instantly rolled onto his back, taking her with him. She stretched out on top of his glistening body, nestling her head in the crook of his neck.

Neither spoke.

Thoughts that might have become words floated lazily into their minds, then were dismissed, none adequate to describe what they had just shared.

So no words were spoken.

But they knew.

Then bodies cooled and heartbeats quieted. Kathy shifted reluctantly off of Dakota but stayed close to his side. He encircled her with one arm, wanting her there.

"Oh, Dakota," she finally whispered.

He kissed her on the forehead. "Yes, I know."

Minutes ticked by, and the sweet bliss of peaceful slumber began to drift over them.

"Dakota?" Kathy said, a sleepy quality to her voice.

"Mmm."

"How could we have shared what we did, something so beautiful, so rare and rich, so honest and real, if your spirit wasn't here with you? Maybe we misinterpreted what we saw in the mirror. You *are* here, Dakota. I would know, now, if you weren't, if a portion of you had been missing."

"The spirit flows through the entire man, Kathy. It's part of him, his heart, his mind, all that he is. But the actual spirit, the essence of who he is, is at his center, the place of his self, his being. Who he is."

"If it flows all through you, then can't you stay here in this time? You *do* have your spirit."

"No, you don't understand. It's like a lake of pure, crystal-clear water that flows out into many streams, nurturing as it goes. But if the center, the lake, disappears and I'm empty, then soon there will be no streams. Now do you see?''

"Yes, I guess I do." She paused. "Dakota, what will happen if you don't go back to where your center spirit is? What will become of you?''

Several minutes passed, but he didn't answer.

Kathy raised her head to look at him. "Dakota? What will happen to you?''

He drew one thumb gently over her lips, then across the soft skin of her cheek, before meeting her troubled gaze.

"Kathy," he said quietly, "I will die."

Six

Kathy stirred, opened her eyes, then frowned as she realized she had no idea where she was.

"Oh," she said in the next instant.

Darkness had fallen, and the sky was a spectacle of beauty with millions of stars glittering like diamonds on black velvet. The luminescence from the heavens made it possible for her to see Dakota, who was sleeping peacefully next to her.

A soft smile touched her lips as she gazed at him, marveling at the power of his magnificent body evident even in slumber.

She shifted slightly and was immediately aware of a foreign yet exquisite soreness in her body that was the result of the lovemaking shared with Dakota.

As vivid, sensual pictures of their joining began to form in her mind's eye, heat began to pulse deep within her. She wanted him again, still, forever.

Forever, her mind echoed, and she frowned. There would be no forever with Dakota.

I will die.

Dear heaven, they had to solve the mystery of the Dream Catcher before it was too late. They had to find a way to send Dakota back to his own time to be united with his spirit.

When he had told her what would happen to him if he remained separated from the center of his spirit, Kathy couldn't speak as unshed tears filled her eyes.

She'd clung to him, holding fast, with the wild, irrational thought that she could keep him with her, safe, if she didn't let go. She'd kissed him, covering his mouth with hers before he could say any more that she couldn't bear to hear.

They were consumed instantly with passion, and all thoughts mercifully fled. Their lovemaking had been urgent, frenzied, with a near-desperate need to become one entity that could not be torn apart by outside forces.

How strange, Kathy mused, still staring at Dakota as he slept, that she could be feeling such joy and such sorrow at the same moment.

She sighed in contentment, allowing the warmth of her happiness to flow through her like a gentle brook.

But then the chill of sadness came, clutching her heart with an icy fist.

I will die.

She hadn't asked Dakota how long they had to discover the hidden magic of the Dream Catcher, because she hadn't been prepared to hear the answer. When he awoke she'd gather her courage and ask the dreaded question.

Dear God, she thought, tears misting her eyes, she didn't want Dakota to leave her. She cared deeply for him, and she wanted to continue on the journey of discovery of what they might ultimately have together.

But he had to go so that he could live. His life was more important than her aching heart, and she would muster all her strength to enable her to bid him farewell with dignity. Somehow.

"Dakota," she said, jiggling his arm, "wake up."

He responded instantly, sitting bolt upward, which caused Kathy to fall back onto the blanket.

"Goodness," she said, "when you wake up, you really do a job of it."

"Mmm."

"We have to leave here." She glanced at her watch. "It's nearly nine o'clock. Clothes. Where are my clothes?" She sat up and began to scoop the garments together.

"I'd like to spend the remainder of the night under the stars," Dakota said, looking heavenward.

"I don't know if this is an official campsite, or what the rules are about that. Besides, it's getting chilly. We'd better go back to the house."

"Kathy, wait."

"Yes?"

"You *do* know that you're my woman, my wife, now, don't you?"

She placed one hand on his forearm.

"No, Dakota," she said gently, "I'm not your wife. We made love. We're lovers. But we're not married. We're not husband and wife."

"Yes, we are. This was our marriage bed and our joining made us one. You're my woman. I'm your man. We're married. That's the way of the Apaches."

Kathy sighed. "But it's not *my* way. To be married, people sign official documents, speak vows before someone authorized to perform the marriage ceremony. Not only that, Dakota, but I would never marry unless I was in love. Unless I was prepared to make a commitment to forever, to spending the rest of my life with my husband.''

"You don't care for me?''

"I care for you very, very much. You've become so important to me so quickly, but I need more time to discover all there is to know about you, to nurture those feelings and see if they grow into love. I can't believe that you love me, either.''

"Caring is enough for marriage,'' he said, his voice rising. "The love comes as days and nights pass. You need time to discover more about me, to nurture the feelings you now have? We don't have a lot of time.''

Kathy got to her feet and began to dress.

"I realize that,'' she said. "I drew on my courage and made the choice to live for the moment we hold in our hands. I have no regrets about what we shared here, none at all. But I'm not your wife, Dakota. We're not married, because I'm not in love with you. Plus, we have no future together, no forever.''

Dakota rolled to his feet and gripped her shoulders.

"You won't honor me as a man by being my wife while I'm here?''

"It has nothing to do with honoring you. I can't, I won't, allow myself to think beyond the moment. You've got to go back to your own time, Dakota.

"Oh, don't you see? It's going to be difficult enough for me when you leave. Somehow, *somehow,* I'm going to make certain I don't fall in love with you. I hope, pray, a person can control their own emotions in the arena of love. Dakota, I am *not* your wife.''

He narrowed his eyes. "You are refusing to acknowledge that we are married? You're dismissing what took place in our marriage bed?"

Kathy stepped backward, forcing him to drop his hands from her shoulders. She continued to dress.

"Please don't do this," she said. "You're spoiling everything by asking more of me than I can give you."

"You gave *yourself* to me." Dakota began to pull on his clothes with rough, angry motions. "Doesn't that mean something to you?"

"Of course it does. I don't take lovemaking lightly. I don't engage in casual sex. Darn it, you were the one who said we should live for the moment, and now you want a lifelong commitment from me. This doesn't make sense, because you know as well as I do that you can't stay here."

"So you'd have me return to my time dishonored, an Apache brave who shared his marriage bed with his woman, only to be told you refuse to be my wife? You would do that to me?"

"Dakota, look, we're arguing about customs and rituals that are different because we come from different worlds, different cultures."

He stopped dressing and looked at her for a long moment.

"Too different," he finally said quietly.

"No, I don't believe that. If you were staying here and if we fell in love, we'd find a way to mesh our worlds. But there's no point in discussing it because you've got to leave. I don't want to spend what time we have left arguing. Please, Dakota? Can't we put this issue of marriage aside, not address it?"

"You don't understand the importance of it. You don't understand *me*."

"And you're not understanding *me*. We haven't had time to make all the discoveries we need to."

"That may be true, *but you are my wife*."

"All right! You follow your customs and consider me your wife. I'll follow mine and know I'm *not* your wife. How's that? Will that do?"

"No!"

Kathy sighed. "We're just going in circles here. If you won't put the issue aside for good, let's at least agree to talk about it later when our tempers are under control. There's something of a far greater magnitude that we should be concentrating on."

"Which is?" he said, still frowning.

Well, Kathy thought miserably, there was no excuse for postponing this any longer.

"Dakota, how long... What I mean is, how much time... That is... Do you know how long we have to figure out how to send you back through the Dream Catcher before you... before you... die?"

He sighed and closed the distance between them, framing her face in his hands.

"No," he said, "I don't know. Once, many years ago, a brave in my tribe lost his wife and two sons to a fever. He grieved deeply. Within days he began to lose the strength in his body, became weak, unable to eat, could hardly walk. The shaman spoke over him to rid him of the sickness holding him."

"What happened?"

"The shaman finally said that the center of the brave's spirit had perished with his wife and sons, and there was no way to stop the remainder of his spirit from flowing out of him. He died, went to his eternal beyond, two weeks after he'd buried his family."

"Oh, God," she whispered.

"That's the only time I witnessed such a happening. I can't say exactly how long I have, because the powers of the Dream Catcher are intertwined. But after what I witnessed those years ago, Kathy, I don't think I have much time. I believe that there are not many days left for us to be together."

"I see," she said, trying desperately to blink away sudden tears. "Well, we certainly don't want to spend those hours arguing, do we? No, of course we don't." She paused. "Come on, Dakota, let's go home."

Home. Let's go home.

The words echoed in Kathy's head as she drove toward the city, envisioning her little cottage in her mind. She'd found such inner peace and contentment in that house during the last year. It was her safe haven, a place that emphasized the rightness of her decision to move from Chicago to Prescott.

But now the mental image of the house after Dakota was gone was a picture of empty rooms and lonely hours.

Let's go home.

Would it still seem like a *home* when Dakota was no longer there? Or would it be just a structure where she slept, ate, spent her leisure time? Would she continue to be capable of accepting as fact what was missing from her life: a husband, children, a *home?*

A flash of anger sliced through her, and her hold on the steering wheel tightened.

Darn it . . . no, *damn it* . . . she wished none of this had happened. She wished Dakota hadn't been transported from the past to the present by the Dream Catcher.

Why her? Many people had purchased Dream Catchers at the craft show, then proceeded blissfully on their way.

But Kathy Maxwell? *Her* Dream Catcher had gone nuts, and because it had she was in the midst of a confusing, unsettling, bizarre mess. If she could turn back the clock, she'd march past the booth of Dream Catchers without a sideward glance.

She sighed.

That wasn't true and she knew it. What had happened with the Dream Catcher was a blessing, not a curse. She would cherish every memory, every precious moment, spent with Dakota.

She knew he had to return to 1877. If he didn't he would die. *Dear heaven, he would die.* He couldn't stay here. Even more, he didn't want to. He viewed their worlds and beliefs as being too different, too far apart. He'd rather exist alone and lonely in his own era.

She'd hurt him by refusing to acknowledge that she was his wife, and his pain had shown itself in the form of anger. They'd each stood their ground, stubbornly declaring that their stand on the subject was the way it should be.

Had she been wrong? Knowing they had to find a way to send Dakota back, should she have graciously accepted the title of his wife for the duration of his stay? No, she couldn't do that, she just couldn't.

Why not? Kathy asked herself. Oh, enough was enough. She was mentally exhausted and just couldn't think anymore tonight. She'd address the issue again later. Fine.

At the house Kathy emptied the hamper, put it away, then sat down on the sofa. Dakota had settled cross-legged on the floor.

"Dakota," she said, "my cousin, Lily, and her husband, Brad, are coming over tomorrow evening to meet you, and to help us try to solve the mystery of how to transport you back to your own time through the Dream Catcher."

"Mmm," he said, nodding.

"Would you like to go to The Herb Hogan with me tomorrow, instead of staying here alone all day?"

He nodded again.

"Oh, Dakota, I'm sorry I hurt you, I truly am. I just can't agree to saying that I'm your wife. Please don't let this issue ruin what time we have left together."

"I'm trying not to, Kathy."

"Thank you." She paused. "It's not all that late, but I think I'll go to bed. Where . . . where do you want to sleep tonight?"

"With you. I wish to sleep with you in our marriage bed."

"Dakota . . ."

He raised one hand to silence her. "I can't view it any other way. I'm not referring to the titles of husband and wife. I am talking only about the bed."

"Which is intertwined with the titles we're not discussing, but so be it." Kathy got up from the sofa. "If you can separate things, then so can I. I don't want anything to tarnish what time we have left."

Dakota rolled to his feet, drew Kathy against him and captured her lips with his. The searing kiss was urgent and rough, his tongue plummeting into her mouth to meet her tongue.

Kathy answered the demands of Dakota's mouth in kind. The hunger, the need, to blot out all that threatened them consumed her with an overwhelming intensity.

She wanted to fly to the place of ecstasy where only she and Dakota could go . . . together. Nothing, nor no one, could intrude upon the private world they created when they were one entity, their bodies meshed.

Dakota broke the kiss and lifted her into his arms, carrying her into the bedroom. He set her on her feet and they quickly shed their clothes, hands immediately reaching for the other once again.

Kathy moved into his embrace, pressing tightly against him as he kissed her. She clung to him, feeling his arousal, meeting his tongue and stroking it, crushing her breasts to the hard wall of his chest.

They tumbled onto the bed, and in one powerful thrust, Dakota entered her. Filling her, he instantly began a pounding rhythm that she met beat for beat. It was wild, like a storm gathering force. It swept them up and away from the threatening truths of reality.

They reached the summit a breath apart, calling to each other, glorying in the splendor of the brightly colored place they'd been flung to. The wildflowers, *their* wildflowers, welcomed them once again.

They lingered there, not wishing to return. Minutes passed as they savored what they'd shared, held fast to what was now another cherished memory.

"Did I hurt you, Kathy?" Dakota said finally. "I was rough when I should have been gentle."

"Oh, no," she said, splaying one hand on his chest, "you didn't hurt me. It was wonderful. When we make love, Dakota, only the two of us exist in the entire universe. We go to *our* place, where no one can find us. I wish there was really somewhere we could hide."

"There isn't."

"I know," she said with a sigh.

"Are you sorry you bought the Dream Catcher that day? Sorry you hung it above your bed? Do you wish I had never come into your life?"

"No, I'm not sorry." She laughed softly. "I tried to be. I attempted to get rip-roaring mad about it, but that lasted about three seconds. If I could turn back the clock to the moment I stood in front of that booth on the square and saw the Dream Catchers, I'd pick the pretty little pink one and hang it carefully above my pillow. Do *you* wish I'd walked on past that booth?"

Dakota shifted so he could look directly into her eyes. "No."

"That's all you have to say on the subject?"

"That's enough."

"Yes," she said, sleepily, "it is."

Holding fast to each other, they slept.

The Herb Hogan was part of the downtown area of Prescott. The row of buildings in the block dated back to the turn of the century with weathered charm.

Inside the store Kathy turned on the lights, flipped the sign on the door to Open, then went behind the counter, placing her purse in a drawer. Dakota stood just inside the door.

Kathy watched him as he swept his gaze slowly over the expanse.

This shop was her pride and joy, she mused, the fulfillment of a dream she'd nurtured until it had become a reality. She was so proud of The Herb Hogan, had made it the focus of her existence, her purpose.

She had dealt with the realization that the trade-off for choosing to live in this delightful little town would very likely be that she would never marry and have children. She refused to settle for any man, just to have a man, and the selection in Prescott was extremely limited. Her maternal instincts would be satisfied by lavishing affection on Lily and Brad's daughters.

She'd not been lonely in her aloneness, and she was prepared to live out her life as it was.

But then . . . Dakota.

Now she knew the meaning of caring deeply for someone, of wanting to discover all and everything about one special man, of sharing and being connected, while still maintaining a sense of self.

Yet as quickly as these wondrous things had come into her life, they were going to be snatched from her grasp when Dakota left her. Oh, dear heaven, the image in her mind's eye of her existence without him was cold, so horribly cold and empty.

Enough, Kathy, she scolded herself. She'd end up thoroughly depressed if she dwelled on the fact that Dakota must return to his own era in history. She'd be so busy feeling sorry for herself that there wouldn't be room in her emotional treasure chest to place each precious memory of the time spent with this man.

She forced her gloomy thoughts into a dusty corner of her mind and watched as Dakota scrutinized The Herb Hogan. She attempted to see it fresh as he was.

The store was bright and cheerful, the gleaming front windows allowing sunlight to pour in. The shelves were dust-free and neat with various bottles, jars, pouches and packets lined up in precise order. Every inch of space had been utilized, but she had been careful not to present an image of overwhelming clutter. There were shelves behind the counter, as well, and a back room beyond a closed door.

Dakota nodded. "This is excellent. I don't know what a lot of these things are, but I recognize others. This is a fine store, Kathy."

Kathy felt a rush of warmth suffuse her from Dakota's praise, and she smiled.

"Thank you," she said. "I'm very proud of The Herb Hogan, and it means a great deal to me that you approve of what I've done."

She paused and frowned. "No, that didn't sound quite right. I'm proud for myself, within myself, for what I've accomplished. I don't need anyone's approval, per se, to affirm what I've done. But your praise is lovely, like a warm, fuzzy blanket. An extra bonus. Do you understand what I'm trying to say?"

Dakota walked slowly across the room and behind the counter, a thoughtful expression on his face.

"What you said is far different than the customs of my people. Women are held in high regard, respected, but the work they do, the tasks they perform, are done for the approval of their fathers, then later their husbands. They're given their worth by those they've hoped to please."

"Mmm," Kathy said, frowning.

"I never questioned it, because it was how it had always been. Yet, now that I think about it, isn't it better that a woman be complete within herself, her spirit whole, as she comes to her man?" He nodded. "Yes, I believe it is."

Kathy slipped her arms around his waist. "Oh, Dakota, do you realize what you just did? You opened your mind to new ideas, a new way of viewing things. It's the way things are here, in this time. That's wonderful."

He encircled her with his arms and pulled her closer to his body.

"It's not really important, Kathy. I can't stay here."

She sighed. "I know. Come into the back area and I'll show you my workroom. You can fill jars, packets and pouches with dried herbs if you want to."

"In a minute," he said, then lowered his head and claimed her mouth.

The smoldering embers of desire within Kathy burst instantly into licking flames as she returned the kiss in total abandon.

The sound of a tinkling bell as the front door was opened caused her to jerk in surprise. She attempted to step free of Dakota's embrace, but he released her slowly, causing a blush of embarrassment to stain her cheeks.

She turned to greet a woman in her mid-thirties, who had entered the store and was staring at Kathy and Dakota with wide eyes.

"Well, my goodness," the woman said, coming to the front of the counter. She smiled at Kathy. "Having a nice day? I'm sorry I interrupted. You'd probably like to strangle me."

"Hi, Sharon," Kathy said, then cleared her throat. "I'd like you to meet Dakota. He's an old . . . friend."

"I'm pleased to meet you, Dakota," Sharon said, beaming at him. "How long do you plan to be in Prescott?"

"I'm not certain," he said.

"Well, maybe you should consider staying here," Sharon went on. "You and Kathy are obviously very glad to see each other." She raised her eyebrows. "Old *friend*? I'm thinking perhaps Kathy is more than just your friend."

"Kathy is my wife," Dakota said.

"Oh, good Lord," Kathy said.

"Wife?" Sharon repeated. Her eyes darted back and forth between Kathy and Dakota.

"Yes," he said, nodding, "but she's reluctant to accept the title, so we're not discussing it to avoid an argument."

"Did that make sense?" Sharon said. "Kathy Maxwell, did you get married and not tell me? Why won't you acknowledge that you're Dakota's wife? Are you on some liberated woman kick or something? Married. I'm so thrilled for you."

"Sharon, wait, halt," Kathy said, raising both hands. "Things aren't exactly as you think they are. What I mean is... Well, Dakota and I... But I really can't explain because... Oh, for crying out loud." She rolled her eyes heavenward.

"Dakota," Sharon said, "is this cute person your wife—" she pointed at Kathy "—or isn't she?"

"She is," he said, folding his arms over his chest.

Kathy closed her eyes and shook her head.

"I love it, I love it." Sharon glanced at her watch. "Darn it, I've got to dash. This weekend is Territorial Days, you know, and I'm on the committee. The town will be packed with tourists, per usual. I've got so many last-minute details to tend to.

"I came to get my usual stash of vitamins, because I'm going to need every ounce of energy I have to get through this event. But that's okay, because I love Territorial Days."

In a flurry of activity, Sharon collected what she wanted from the shelves, dumped them onto the counter, then after paying for the purchases, scooped up the bag Kathy had put them in.

"I'm off," Sharon said. "Listen, as soon as Territorial Days are over, we'll talk about a wedding party for you and Dakota. Fantastic." She looked at Dakota.

"You were pulling my leg about not knowing how long you're staying in Prescott, you bum. Of course you're here for good. You're Kathy's husband."

Dakota frowned. "I didn't touch your leg."

"What?" she said, obviously confused.

"Don't worry about it, Sharon," Kathy said wearily. "Have a nice day."

"You, too. I'm off. Are you two coming to Territorial Days? Of course you are. Everybody does. Bye, guys, and best wishes. Married. I love it." She hurried out the door.

As the sound of the tinkling bell above the door faded, an oppressive silence settled over The Herb Hogan. Kathy took a deep breath, let it out slowly, then turned to face Dakota. He still had his arms crossed on his chest, and Kathy lifted her chin to a determined tilt.

Do not yell, she told herself. She would slowly and patiently explain to Dakota what was on her mind, what she needed to say. Fine.

"Dakota," she said, attempting to produce a smile that didn't materialize, "you really shouldn't have told Sharon that I'm your wife."

He frowned as he looked at her. "Why not? You *are* my wife. Why would I deny the truth? You may feel differently about it, but I spoke what is true to me. Honesty is very important to me, Kathy."

"Of course it is, and it's important to me, too. It's a major part of my value system. I'm not suggesting that you lie, but sometimes the truth is better left unsaid. You and I don't agree on the subject of my being, or not being, your wife. Therefore, you should have kept silent. Understand?"

"No."

"Dakota," she said with a sigh, "the news flash that you and I are married will spread through Prescott like a prairie fire. People are going to come streaming in here with a zillion questions. How long have we known each other? Where did we meet? When were we married? Where do we plan to live? Are you going to be running The Herb Hogan with me? And on and on."

Dakota shrugged. "We'll answer only the questions we wish to. We'll say we shared our marriage bed, joined, made love. I see you as my wife, but you don't view me as your husband. That's clear enough."

"Oh, good grief. Dakota, listen to me. Even if I *did* consider myself your wife, it would be foolish to tell people that we're married, because you can't stay here. After you're gone..." Oh, what a chilling word...*gone*. "Everyone will be wanting to know where you went, why you didn't stay with me. They'll look at me and wonder what's so wrong with me that caused my new husband to disappear. Do you see what I mean?"

"Are you saying," he said, his voice ominously low, "that what other people think is of more value to you than honesty, truth?"

Kathy opened her mouth to retort, then snapped it closed again.

Mercy, she thought, Dakota's interpretation of what she had said was *not* flattering. It made her sound cold and superficial, placing her public image higher on her list of importance than honesty.

That wasn't true.

Was it?

No, no, no, it wasn't. Dakota just didn't understand how it was in this era. Things weren't so complex in his time, his place in history. These days a person had to...

"Oh, dear," she said, massaging her now-throbbing temples.

She was becoming all muddled up again. So confused. In this era...what? she asked herself. Honesty only came first if it was convenient, if it wouldn't rock the boat? At the first sign of trouble, were truth and honesty quickly shoved aside by outright lies, or lies of omission? Was that what she was attempting to get across to Dakota, and urging him to agree to?

Yes.

"Dakota," she said quietly, "I'm sorry. I humbly apologize for asking you to do something that's so very wrong, asking you to deny what to you is the truth. I'll deal with the ramifications of what you told Sharon as they come. I won't attempt to change you. You've taught me a great deal by just being you. I thank you for that, and I *am* truly sorry."

Before Dakota could reply, the door opened and two women in their sixties entered The Herb Hogan.

"Hello, Olive, Alida," Kathy said, smiling. "You must be running low on your teas and lotions."

"We are, indeed," Olive said, "but we would have stopped in, anyway. We just bumped into Sharon and she said..."

"Yes," Kathy interrupted, "I'm sure she did. Ladies, I'd like you to meet Dakota. In his world, his culture, we're married. In mine, we're not."

"Pardon me?" Olive said.

"That is all we have to say on the subject," Dakota said, looking directly into Kathy's blue eyes. "Is this compromise?"

"Yes," she said, smiling at him warmly. "This is compromise."

Seven

Business was steady through the day at The Herb Hogan. As the hours passed, more people heard about Dakota's sudden presence in Kathy's life and the rather confusing explanation being given as to the status of their relationship. Most left the store with purchases and bemused expressions.

In the late afternoon, Dakota sat at the table in the back room, filling pouches with various dried herbs.

He was amazingly relaxed, he realized, and had been during the entire day.

Once he'd stopped tensing each time the door opened and someone entered the store, he'd begun to look forward to observing each new person. The diversity in their clothing, coloring, even the way they spoke, was intriguing.

And all of them had smiled and greeted him with sincere warmth.

It was as Kathy had told him; he was safe here, no one was searching for him to kill or capture him. He was being accepted simply as a man. Kathy's man.

Was that why he had been transported here by the Dream Catcher? Had the gods decreed that he wasn't to spend his remaining days like a hunted animal and hurled him forward in time to a place where he was accepted?

If that was true, why had Kathy been intertwined in the process of giving him a new life? And if it was true, why had his center spirit not come with him? Why was he being forced to find a way back to his era?

"Mmm," he said, frowning.

A new life. A *temporary* new life. If he stayed here, he would die. So what had been the purpose for all of this? It made no sense, none at all.

Except...

Kathy.

He liked her smile, the sky blue of her eyes, the sunshine color of her hair. He valued her honesty and sincerity, respected her ability to work in harmony with nature when growing the herbs in the garden. She was a fine woman among women.

He did, indeed, consider her his wife. Their joining was satisfying beyond measure. When they were one entity, it was exquisite. She gave of herself willingly, totally, each time they came together.

He rejoiced in seeing her naked before him, and touching, tasting, every inch of her soft skin. Her breasts were lush, and one day his son would suckle there, receiving the nourishment of mother's milk. He would...

His son?

Dakota snorted in self-disgust. Such foolishness to be envisioning Kathy bearing his son. His stay in this world was going to be brief, not long enough to witness his seed growing bigger within Kathy, producing a fine, healthy boy.

He had to leave here.

He would never see Kathy again.

That thought caused a knot to tighten in his gut, and Dakota shifted on the chair. The hot coil that had swept through him as he dwelled on the lovemaking he shared with Kathy was now a cold current consuming him, clutching his heart in an icy fist.

Oh, why, why had he been brought here to this haven of peace, found the woman he now considered his wife, and yearned to have her grow big with his child, only to be forced to return to a hostile, lonely existence in order to live? Why were the gods tormenting him like this, teasing him so cruelly?

Was this the way it was meant to be? Was he being given a reprieve, a rest, from his world to restore his strength? Were the differences between his beliefs and Kathy's too great for him to remain here forever?

So many questions, he thought, shaking his head. So many answers that remained beyond his reach.

Dakota sighed and reached for another pouch.

Kathy finished recording the totals from the cash register in a ledger, put it away, then crossed the room to lock the door. She flipped the sign to Closed, then wrapped her hands around her elbows. Taking a deep breath, she allowed the silence to cascade over her like a comforting blanket.

As the hours of the day had passed, she mused, she'd become more and more gloomy, finally ending up thoroughly depressed. Her initial joy when she and Dakota had compromised on the issue of her being, or not being, his wife had slowly dissipated until it was completely gone.

They were so very different in their beliefs. Their worlds and cultures were miles apart. How many compromises could two people put into operation and expect them to work? How many were *too* many, creating far too much tension and stress? It was a disturbing, unsettling question.

But her depression, Kathy knew, had hit her full force when she realized the elusive answer didn't matter, because Dakota couldn't remain there. He had to go back to his own time. *He had to.*

Oh, dear heaven, she wanted him to stay.

She *needed* him to stay.

Stop it, Kathy, she ordered herself. She would *not* let her mind travel down the road it was approaching. She would *not* dwell on what she and Dakota might have if he didn't leave. She would *not* entertain the idea that she might eventually fall deeply and forever in love with him.

No!

She shook her head sharply in an attempt to clear her mind of her jumbled thoughts, then headed for the back room to tell Dakota it was time to go home.

Home, her mind echoed. Forget it. She wasn't going to start thinking about home versus house again. She was depressed enough, thank you very much.

After a dinner of hamburgers and French fries, which Dakota declared to have merit, Kathy shooed him into the living room so she could make a dessert to serve to Lily and Brad.

At seven o'clock the doorbell rang and Kathy hurried to answer the summons, greeting Lily and Brad as she opened the door.

As the pair came into the house, Kathy gave them a quick hug. Brad Benson was about five-foot-ten, trim, wore glasses, and was slowly losing his hair, a fact he didn't care one whit about. He was rather nondescript until he smiled. Then his entire face lit up and his eyes twinkled. Kathy adored him.

"Lily and Brad," Kathy said, "I'd like you to meet Dakota."

They all turned toward Dakota, who was standing across the room.

"Oh, my stars," Lily said, awe evident in her voice. "You didn't do him justice. He's . . . Gracious me. This is, indeed, a pleasure, Dakota."

"Pleased to meet you," Brad said, smiling. "You had quite a journey to arrive here, Dakota. Welcome to our world. It must seem very strange to you."

"I'm being rude," Lily said. "I'd like to welcome you, too, Dakota. All of this—" she swept one arm in the air "—must be rather overwhelming."

Dakota walked slowly forward to stand directly in front of Lily.

"Ever since I was a small boy," he said, "I have known if a woman carried a girl child or a boy. The shaman in my tribe told me it was a gift, but I found it a nuisance when I was young because the women would pester me to tell them what the babe within them would be."

"Really?" Lily said, smiling. She patted her stomach. "Well, this is a boy. Guaranteed."

"What would you do to determine the sex of the child?" Brad asked.

"Place my hand gently on the woman's stomach," Dakota said.

"Lily?" Brad said. "How about it? Would you like Dakota to check out your boy theory?"

"Go right ahead, Dakota," Lily said. "This will prove that women know what's going on. This baby is a boy."

Dakota lifted one hand and splayed it on Lily's large stomach. A moment later he nodded.

"You will have," he said, dropping his hand to his side, "a fine, healthy daughter very soon."

"Daughter?" Lily said. "It's a boy, I'm sure of it. Did you ever make a mistake, Dakota?"

He shook his head.

Brad hooted with laughter. "Lily, if I was a betting man I'd put my money on what Dakota said. It's another cute-as-a-button baby girl."

"But I want a boy!"

"Perhaps your next child will be a son," Dakota said.

"Oh, no, you don't," Lily said. "There aren't going to be any more babies after this one."

Dakota frowned. "You're going to refuse to join with your husband? He'll have no choice but to take a second wife."

"Dakota," Kathy said, "that's not how it works now. Lily didn't mean she was planning to refuse to... Oh, good grief, let's all sit down, shall we?"

Lily sat in a straight-backed chair that Brad brought to her from the kitchen table. He settled in a rocking chair, and Kathy and Dakota took places on the sofa.

"Kathy," Lily said, "Sharon called me just before we left the house and said..."

"Yes, yes, I know what she said," Kathy interrupted. "Dakota and I have been dealing all day with the issue of whether or not I'm his wife."

"Well?" Lily said. "Are you his wife?"

"Yes," Dakota said.

"No," Kathy said. "Let's not get into that right now, okay? That's not the issue at hand. We know why we're here. We have to find a way to send Dakota back through the Dream Catcher to his own time."

"Why?" Lily said. "Why can't he stay? You like it here, don't you, Dakota?"

He nodded. "Mmm."

"So," Lily said, throwing up her hands, "stay."

Yes, yes, yes, Kathy's heart sang.

"No," she said, "he can't."

"Why not?" Brad said seriously.

"Because of the mirror," Kathy said.

She quickly related what had happened when she and Dakota had stood in front of the mirror, and Dakota's explanation of what it meant.

"I see," Brad said. "I'm sorry to hear that."

"This is terrible," Lily said.

A heavy silence fell over the room as gazes shifted from one person to the next, each seeking but not finding, a solution to the dilemma. Brad finally spoke.

"Dakota," he said, "if it got right down to it and the choice was yours, would you choose to go back to 1877, or stay here?"

Kathy was hardly breathing as she looked at Dakota, waiting to hear his answer. Seconds ticked by that seemed like hours.

"Apaches face the truth as it is," Dakota said. "Do I wish to go? Stay? It does not matter. I *must* return to my own time to be united with my spirit."

"You'd make a good attorney," Brad said, smiling. "You don't allow your facts to be swayed by emotions, your personal feelings."

"Just for the record, though," Lily said, "would you prefer to stay or go?"

Dakota turned his head to look directly at Kathy. Her heart skipped a beat as she saw the warmth and tenderness in the ebony depths of his eyes.

"I would choose to stay," he said quietly.

Oh, dear heaven, Kathy thought. Oh, Dakota.

"Then we have to find a way to make that possible," Lily said. "We have to. Brad, think of something."

"I need some time to analyze this," Brad said, "to give it more thought. Well, let's take a look at this Dream Catcher of yours."

The group got to their feet and started toward the bedroom.

Dakota wanted to stay, Kathy's mind echoed. He wanted to stay with *her*. Was that wonderful? Or was it terrifying? What exactly were his feelings toward her? He considered her his wife, said caring was enough to get married, and that love would grow as days and nights passed. But was he considering the conflicts between them, the obstacles they faced?

Oh, what difference did it really make? Dakota could *not* stay with her. He was going to leave. She'd be alone. And she would cry.

In the bedroom, Kathy and Dakota slowly and carefully slid the Dream Catcher from beneath the bed.

"My stars," Lily said, "that's unbelievable. I saw you buy it when it was so small, Kathy, and look at it now. Incredible."

"I know," she said.

"Amazing," Brad said.

They pushed the Dream Catcher gently back into its safe place.

"Well, there's obviously no instant solution here," Kathy said, "but at least we'll know you two are thinking about it. Four minds are better than two. Let's go have some dessert."

They were soon sitting around the kitchen table enjoying cherry cobbler topped with dollops of whipped cream. Kathy registered a tremendous sense of pride at how well Dakota managed his spoon.

It was as though he'd used utensils for years, she thought. And it was as though he'd been a part of her life forever.

"Delicious, Kathy," Brad said, leaning back in his chair. "Thank you." He paused. "Well, we need a plan of action. I have a fairly light day scheduled tomorrow. I'll go to the library and see what I can find out about Dream Catchers. I doubt seriously that there's any documentation on an episode like what happened to Dakota actually taking place. But there might be something on the beliefs surrounding the thing."

"If this had happened before," Lily said, "and was made public knowledge, it would have been in every newspaper in the country.

"I shudder to think what it would have been like for the poor person who had been transported here. He wouldn't have a moment's peace or privacy. The press would hound him unmercifully, as well as scientists, historians, even government agents, for all we know. We *must* protect Dakota from that sort of thing."

"Good point," Brad said. "Secrecy is extremely important."

"Sharon asked me what Dakota's last name was," Lily said. "I told her it slipped my mind. She thinks I'm a dunce."

"Native Americans of Dakota's era didn't have last names," Brad said, "but we'd best give you one, Dakota. We want you to appear as though you're a regular citizen. Smith. Dakota Smith. How's that?"

"Two names for one man," he said, smiling. "I'm adopting many of the white man's ways."

Oh, that sinful smile, Kathy thought. He didn't use it often, but when he did, it curled her toes.

"Dakota Smith?" Lily said. "Really, Brad, don't you have more imagination than that? Smith is so boring, ordinary. Dakota is *not* ordinary."

No joke, Kathy thought dryly.

"Smith will do fine, Lily," Brad said. "If you want to spend time dwelling on names, you'd do well to decide on one for our soon-to-be-here daughter. Calling her Michael Bradley Benson isn't going to cut it."

"*She* was supposed to be a *he*," Lily said.

"No," Dakota said. "You don't carry a son. Not this time."

"Don't start *that* again, Dakota Smith," Lily said. "This is the *last* time."

"Mmm," he said. "Perhaps."

Lily glared at him, Brad chuckled, and Kathy fought against threatening tears.

Oh, look at this, she thought, swallowing past the lump in her throat. There they sat, all of them, sharing dessert around the kitchen table. They were comfortable together, a family, two couples: Lily and Brad, Kathy and Dakota. Anyone peering in the window would see a lovely scene.

How empty that chair where Dakota sat would seem when he was gone. How empty her life would be. *Oh, Kathy, please, just stop it.*

"Well, we'd better go," Brad said. "I'll let you know what I find out in the library. Lily, are you ready to take that baby girl home and set the sitter free from the clutches of our other daughters?"

Lily patted her stomach. "So much for Michael Bradley. Oh, well, sugar-and-spice little girls are certainly wonderful. Do you like the name Julie? Susan? Tracey? How about..."

"It's home and bed for you, madam," Brad said, getting to his feet.

Goodbyes were said at the door, then Kathy turned to look at Dakota.

"Well," she said, smiling, "I hope you liked Lily and Brad."

Dakota nodded. "Yes. They're real, honest, with no false fronts."

"Yes, they are." She cocked her head slightly to one side, a thoughtful expression on her face. "You can tell if someone is being open and honest with you, can't you?"

He nodded again. "In my time, having that ability can mean the difference between life or death. It can mean trading and bartering to provide for my people, or being fooled and giving what I have, with not enough gained in return.

"I refused to go to the reservation because I didn't believe the false promises of a prosperous and comfortable life in another place. The soldiers weren't speaking the truth and I knew it. The Apaches are a proud and brave people, but at that moment they were exhausted and frightened. They couldn't hear me when I spoke. And so, they went."

"I'm so sorry, Dakota."

"I stood hidden in the trees and watched them go, my heart heavy, my spirit filled with sorrow. As they disappeared, leaving only the stirred dust in the air, I heard the call of an owl. That sound, that bad omen, was the final proof that my people would never again be free."

Kathy closed the distance between them and placed one hand on his arm.

"They're free now, Dakota," she said softly, "just as I told you. Does that ease your pain, even a little?"

He covered her hand with his. "Yes, it does, and I thank you. You give me many gifts, Kathy."

The gentleness in their eyes as they continued to look at each other began to shift and change. The embers of desire within them glowed brighter, then burst into flames of heated passion.

Invisible threads of sensuality wove around them, encasing them in a cocoon where only they could be. It was their safe haven, where no one could intrude, where the reality of what they faced could not touch them.

"You would really stay here if you could?" Kathy whispered.

"I would stay." He drew his thumb over her lips. "I would stay here with you, my wife."

Kathy knew in the far recesses of her mind that she should voice objection once again to the title of wife that Dakota insisted on giving her. But that knowledge was clouded by the sensual mist consuming her ability to reason.

No, she couldn't think. Not now. It had been a long and exhausting day, and she just couldn't think anymore. She could only feel. She was awash with desire, the heat of it burning low within her, pulsing with a tempo as wild as the beating of her heart.

She felt cherished, respected, appreciated for doing nothing more than being. There was no question as to the honesty of what he was saying, for he knew no other way to speak. He was honoring her with the title of being his wife, and that was a precious gift she would treasure always.

Reality seemed to suddenly tap her on the shoulder, bringing her from her sensuous haze.

"Dakota," she said, "why would you wish to stay here with me as your wife? You were the one who said our worlds were too different, that they couldn't be meshed."

"I spoke those words in anger. I've since seen the merit of compromise. I believe you care deeply enough for me to be my wife. I'm content with that. You need more before accepting the title of wife. You have to be in love with me. That's your right and I respect it." He nodded. "Compromise."

"I see," she said thoughtfully.

"There's nothing left for me in my time, Kathy. Everything I had, who I was, has been stripped away. It no longer exists. Here? I have you, people who accept me, and I don't have to fear for my life."

"But what about all the other differences between us, our cultures, our worlds? I know I said that compromising could solve all of our problems, but now I wonder if that's really true. How many compromises can a relationship withstand?"

"What are *all these differences* that you refer to?"

"Oh, well, you know, like..." Kathy stopped speaking and frowned. "There's a whole list of them, but I'm too tired to click them off right now."

"A list."

"Yes."

"Is there? Are you positive of that?" Dakota sighed. "This conversation is useless. I have to go back, and we both know that. I wish I knew why I was transported here by the Dream Catcher. To come, then be forced to leave, makes no sense to me. I don't regret it, but I don't understand it."

"There's a great many things I don't understand," Kathy said wearily. "I'm so exhausted."

"Then let's go to bed and get the rest we need. I don't have the energy I'm accustomed to. It's flowing out of me and there's no center spirit to replenish it."

"Oh, Dakota, I . . ."

"Hush. No more talking tonight. It's been a long, tiring day."

Several hours later, Kathy lay wide wake next to a sleeping Dakota. Despite her fatigue, she was unable to sleep, to shut off the cacophony of jumbled thoughts that chased each other in an endless, tangled circle in her mind.

Why *had* the Dream Catcher brought Dakota here and left his spirit behind? What had been the true purpose of all of this?

She shifted into a more comfortable position, willing herself to allow sleep to claim her.

When Dakota had asked her what obstacles stood in the way of their being together, her mind had been a complete blank. There *was* a list of differences between them, potential sources of problems.

Kathy yawned.

So, okay, she hadn't been able to say what they were when Dakota had pressed for an answer. That made sense because she was so tired. She'd remember them in the morning.

Wouldn't she?

Eight

In the light of the new day, Kathy decided that dwelling
on the list of reasons why she and Dakota could not have
a future together was a waste of valuable mental energy.

The issue that had to be focused on was how to transport Dakota back to 1877. He was already experiencing
the physical effects of his spirit flowing from his body.

They were rapidly running out of time.

In the late morning, Lily came into The Herb Hogan
for a quick hello, saying she wouldn't stay long as she
had the two youngest girls with her. They possessed, she
declared, the busiest fingers in the West and were haz-
ardous to the health of Kathy's store.

Lily had received several more telephone calls from
people inquiring if it was true that Kathy was married,
and asking Lily for the juicy details.

"I winged it," she said merrily, after Kathy had exclaimed over how far the story had spread. "Due to the fact *I* was confused, I've probably thoroughly confused everyone else. Knowing me, I didn't say the same thing twice. Oh, well."

"There will be a new piece of gossip by tomorrow," Kathy said. "Dakota and I will be old news."

"However," Lily said, pointing one finger in the air, "do remember that our mothers are planning to fly in from Florida when this baby is born. They're not going to be put off as easily as folks here. They'll be into when, where and how in a big way, and most definitely will demand a straight answer regarding your marital status."

"Oh, good grief," Kathy said, rolling her eyes heavenward. "Don't have the baby too soon, Lily. I have to think about what I'm going to tell them."

"Oh, okay," Lily said, laughing and patting her stomach. "The message has been sent to this human cargo. *She* has been told. Dakota, are you absolutely positive that I'm carrying a girl?"

"Mmm," he said, nodding.

"Since you wanted to name a boy Michael," Kathy said, "why don't you call the new baby Michelle?"

"That's a thought," Lily said. "Holly, no, no, sweetheart, don't touch Aunt Kathy's pretty bottles. Come on, girls, we've got to go."

"Lily, wait," Kathy said. "Have you talked to Brad? He was planning to go the library to investigate Dream Catchers."

"No, I haven't talked to him since this morning but I'm sure he'll be in touch with you later. Bye for now."

Just minutes before closing time, Brad entered the store.

"Hi, Brad," Kathy said. "Would you lock the door and flip the sign to Closed, please?"

Brad did as instructed, then came to the counter.

"I waited until now to come by so we wouldn't be interrupted," he said.

"Good idea. Let's go into the back room and sit down," Kathy said.

Settled on chairs at the table in the rear area, Kathy and Dakota looked at Brad questioningly.

"Well, I have good news and bad news," Brad said. "The bad is that the reference material at the library was about what I expected. The history and legend of the Dream Catcher is fully documented. I even found instructions for how to make them. There was nothing to help us with your situation, though, Dakota."

"And the good news?" Kathy said, leaning slightly toward Brad.

"I found an article about Dream Catchers written by a Dr. John Tucker. He's a professor, retired from Northern Arizona University, and he still lives in Flagstaff. He taught courses for many years on native American history, culture, folklore, customs, the whole enchilada."

"The what?" Dakota said.

"Oh, sorry, Dakota," Brad said. "The man knows a great deal about Indians. The thing is, there was a subtle message in the article that Indian folklore should not be taken lightly, that it was not given the proper respect. I got the distinct feeling that this Dr. Tucker truly believes in many of the legends."

"And?" Kathy said.

"I took a chance and called him. Oh, yes, indeed, the good professor believes in Indian legends. I crossed my fingers, hoped I wasn't making a mistake, and told him how Dakota had gotten here."

"Oh, dear," Kathy said, reaching over to grasp Dakota's hand.

"Dr. Tucker didn't flicker. He was excited about what I was saying, was totally accepting, and said it was bound to have happened eventually since the surge of popularity of people owning Dream Catchers. He was surprised it hadn't occurred before now."

"I'll be darned," Kathy said.

"Can he be trusted?" Dakota said.

"Yes," Brad said. "He understands the importance of secrecy, said he cringed at the thought of what would happen to Dakota if this became known publicly."

"Brad, did you explain to him about Dakota's center spirit not traveling through the Dream Catcher with him?" Kathy said.

Brad nodded, then sighed. "Dr. Tucker said that you can't survive here, Dakota, without the center of your spirit."

"I know," Dakota said.

Kathy tightened her hold on his hand.

"Did Dr. Tucker say what we should do to return Dakota to his own time?" Kathy said. Oh, no, please, no. She didn't want him to leave her.

"He's going to do some research on it," Brad said. "He knows a great many native Americans and can ask questions about the Dream Catcher, without them wondering why he's interested, because he's gathered data from them for many years."

"When will you be speaking with him again?" Kathy asked.

"He and his wife are coming over on Saturday for Territorial Days. Dr. Tucker is very eager to meet Dakota, and we're to connect with them at Sharlot Hall at two in the afternoon. I'll recognize him because his picture was printed with the article.''

"This is only Wednesday, Brad," Kathy said. "There are precious days being wasted until Saturday.''

"Dr. Tucker will call if he discovers something before Saturday. He realizes that time is of the essence, but he feels he's in for a real challenge as far as finding out what we have to know. He needs the days until Saturday, if not longer.''

"We don't know how much longer Dakota has," Kathy said, her voice trembling.

"Calm down, Kathy," Dakota said. "Brad has done all he can, and I'm grateful for that. We will have to be patient until we can meet with Dr. Tucker.''

"I didn't come equipped with Apache patience," she said, sighing. "Thank you so much for everything you did today, Brad.''

Brad got to his feet. "Well, we'll see what happens on Saturday. I'd better get home to my harem.''

Kathy and Dakota stood and the two men shook hands. Brad left the store, and a few minutes later Kathy and Dakota were driving toward her house. Neither spoke, each digesting all that Brad had said.

Inside the house, Kathy started toward the bedroom.

"I'm going to change into jeans," she said, "then I'll fix dinner.''

She stopped suddenly, turned, and hurried back to where Dakota was still standing in the middle of the living room. She wrapped her arms tightly around his waist, looking up at him.

"I want to hold fast to you," she said, unable to keep tears from filling her eyes, "to somehow keep you safe.

I'm so worried that we won't find the answers we need in time.''

Dakota encircled her slender body with his arms.

"We have to hope that Dr. Tucker will discover the mysteries of the Dream Catcher, and send me back so I can be united with my center spirit.''

"Dakota, what if... what if we asked Dr. Tucker if there is a way to transport your spirit from there to here? If he discovers how to send you back to your spirit, doesn't it make sense that he could do it in reverse?'' She rested her head on his chest.

"Yes,'' he said, "I suppose. There's no harm in asking him.''

But a frown knitted his brows, and an expression of deep sadness settled over his features. He buried his face in Kathy's silky curls and tightened his hold on her, not wanting to let her go. Wishing to stay with her in her world. Forever.

Hours later, just before Kathy drifted off to sleep, she nestled closer to Dakota, placing one hand on his chest to feel the beat of his heart beneath her palm. He was asleep, the steady rise and fall of his chest giving her a sense of well-being.

They had both executed maximum effort to push aside the cloud of gloom and fear hovering over them so they could enjoy the evening together.

Kathy had laughed in delight at Dakota's shock as he tasted ice cream for the first time. After his second bowl, he declared the dessert to have great merit.

They'd weeded and watered the herb garden, removed some of the dried herbs that were ready to go to The Herb Hogan from the drying wall, then watched a movie on television.

And then they'd made love, Kathy remembered dreamily. It had been exquisite, so beautiful. Nothing was allowed to intrude into their private world of ecstasy, of sharing, of being one glorious entity.

Kathy closed her eyes and slept.

Early the next afternoon, a man entered The Herb Hogan with several small rugs draped over one arm. Kathy greeted him pleasantly.

"The name is Sam Spander," the man said. "I'm down from Nevada to have a booth on the square for Territorial Days. I came in early to make the rounds of the merchants, give you a chance to sell authentic Navajo rugs out of your own stores. I have enough other inventory to allow you to deal in the rugs."

"They're lovely," Kathy said.

Sam spread the rugs out on the counter.

"I can let you have them at a good price. I have some Navajos who weave these exclusively for me. Authentic Navajo rugs are hard to come by, but I have a steady supply. Are you interested?"

"Well . . ." Kathy said, staring at the pretty rugs.

"No," Dakota said, then folded his arms tightly over his chest.

"Dakota?" Kathy said, looking at him in surprise. "Mr. Spander, this is Dakota Smith."

"I'm Apache," Dakota said.

"Nice to meet you," Sam said, eyeing him warily.

"Kathy doesn't want your rugs," Dakota said.

"I don't?" she said. "Why don't I?"

"Because those were not made by Navajos," Dakota said, a steely edge to his voice.

"Now, wait just a damn minute," Sam said.

"Dakota," Kathy said, "how do you know these aren't authentic Navajo rugs?"

Dakota pointed to the end of one of the rugs.

"They have fringe. Navajos weave with one continuous strand on a loom. Their rugs are smooth on all sides, and never have fringe. The Navajo's prayer is 'to walk in beauty,' and they make rugs with no frills, no fringe. They are an expression of simplistic beauty. No, these are not Navajo rugs."

"Well, well, Sam," Kathy said, "now what do you have to say?"

Dakota narrowed his eyes as he looked at Sam. "You've tried to cheat my woman, my wife. An Apache brave doesn't stand silently by and allow such a thing to happen."

Sam's eyes widened in fright. "Now, don't get excited, Dakota...Mr. Smith." He snatched up the rugs and began to back toward the door. "This is just a little misunderstanding, that's all. I'll get out of your way. No problem."

"Leave Prescott before the sun sets," Dakota said.

Sam stopped in his tracks. "I've paid for a booth on the square for the weekend."

"No," Dakota said. "You'll be gone. You won't cheat people in this town, or diminish the honor of the Navajo by presenting inferior rugs as being made by them. Do you understand me?"

"You bet. I'm gone. Out of town," Sam said, turning toward the door. "You never saw me." He hurried out of the store.

Kathy burst into laughter. "Oh, Dakota, you were wonderful. Did you see his face? I think he had images of your scalping him, or some grim thing."

"Mmm," Dakota said, still frowning. "No one will treat my wife poorly. If they do, they answer to me."

"My hero," Kathy said, smiling at him warmly.

"Your husband," Dakota said with a decisive nod.

An hour later, Kathy received a telephone call from one of her homebound customers, requesting a new supply of the herbs she used for brewing tea, as well as her favorite lotion. Kathy promised to deliver the products after regular working hours.

She went into the back room where Dakota was filling pouches with herbs, and explained that they'd drive to the woman's house before going home for dinner.

"Oh, you're filling pouches with cinnamon tea," she said. "I recommend it for morning sickness, among other things."

Dakota looked up at her. "Tea brewed from the root of the ginger plant is best for the sickness at dawn that comes with carrying a child."

"Gingerroot?" Kathy said, frowning. "That's for ailments resulting from circulation problems."

Dakota shrugged. "It's used by my people for the dawn sickness."

"Let me look it up in my reference book."

"Kathy," Dakota said, his voice very low, "*I* have said that gingerroot is what is best for dawn sickness."

"And *I*," Kathy said, her blue eyes flashing with anger, "have never heard of it being used for that."

She went to the front, then returned with a large book that she thunked onto the table. After shooting Dakota a stormy glare, she began to flip quickly through the pages until coming to the *G* section.

"Ginger," she muttered, drawing one fingertip down the column of small print. "Ginger, ginger. Ah, here we go. Gingerroot." She quickly read the information, her eyes widening. "Oh."

"Oh?" Dakota said.

A flush of embarrassment stained Kathy's cheeks.

"Gingerroot tea *is* used to relieve morning sickness," she said. "Well, Dakota, I'm sorry. You were right and I apologize."

Dakota got to his feet and crossed his arms over his chest, frowning deeply. "An Apache wife would never question the words of her husband. It doesn't demonstrate the proper respect due a man. You shouldn't have doubted what I said to you."

Anger erupted in Kathy like a volcano. She opened her mouth, realized she was so furious she was unable to string two words together, and looked like a puffing goldfish. She snapped her mouth closed, then turned to the table and began to drum her fingertips on the surface in an erratic rhythm.

"Did you understand me, Kathy?" Dakota said, a cold edge to his voice.

That did it.

She spun around, her blue eyes flashing like laser beams.

"Don't you dare speak to me in that tone of voice, Dakota Smith. You're talking to me the same way you did to that sleazeball with the phony rugs. Don't even think about doing a 'me Tarzan, you Jane' routine on me."

"Who?"

"Forget that part," she said, flipping one hand in the air. "Dakota, women in this era have a voice."

Dakota stared at her for a moment, then laughed. "A *loud* voice. All right, Kathy, you've definitely made your point."

"I did?" She blinked. "Well, fancy that." She matched his smile. "This is a perfect situation for some culture training. You see, Dakota, when two people have an argument, they holler a tad, end the nonsense, then make up."

"Oh?"

"Yes, indeed. This is very important."

"What's this making-up process?"

"Well," she said, "I'll demonstrate it for you, sort of like show-and-tell."

She wrapped her arms around his neck, molded herself to his rugged body, and covered his mouth with hers in a searing kiss. Dakota encircled her with his arms and returned the kiss in total abandon, meeting her questing tongue eagerly with his own.

Kathy sank her hands into his thick, silky hair, urging his mouth harder onto hers, savoring his taste, the feel of his aroused body pressed against her, inhaling his special aroma.

When she finally ended the kiss, they stayed locked in each other's embrace. Desire radiated from Dakota's obsidian eyes, matching the ardor shining in Kathy's blue eyes.

"This making-up has merit," Dakota said, his voice raspy.

"Great, huh?" Kathy laughed. "Make love, not war." She nestled her head on his chest and sighed in contentment.

They stood silently for a long moment, savoring.

"Kathy?" Dakota finally said.

"Yes?"

"Who is Tarzan?"

* * *

"This will be fun, Dakota," Kathy said as they drove away from The Herb Hogan. "The delivery I'm making is on a side of town you haven't seen yet. So, sir, I'll be your tour guide."

Dakota chuckled.

"Oh, do you understand about traffic lights?" Kathy said, pressing on the brake.

"You've stopped because the red light came on. When the green one glows, you'll start off again. The yellow in the middle means you press your foot harder on the pedal and race forward before it changes to red."

"Oh, dear, shame on me. Some people stop the instant they see the yellow light, but I... Never mind, that's boring. Now, then, on your left is the old armory, which is ancient and constructed of stone. Isn't it marvelous? It's used for all kinds of activities. It has a gymnasium where people play basketball and stuff, take classes in dancing, aerobics, martial arts and..."

Kathy chattered on, directing Dakota's attention to the left, right, then back to the left. He couldn't understand all the words she was using, but didn't interrupt for definitions. Kathy looked so happy, her blue eyes sparkling, and he enjoyed looking at her far more than the landmarks.

After the delivery to the homebound customer had been made, Kathy drove away from the woman's house. A beautiful sunset was just beginning to streak across the sky in vibrant colors, acting as a backdrop to the mountains in the distance. The air was clear and clean, and a cool breeze carried an aroma of flowers and freshly cut grass.

Kathy glanced over at Dakota, smiling at the mere sight of him, then paid attention to the traffic again.

"Have you had enough commentary for now?" she said. "Oh, one last thing. On the right up ahead is the Veterans Hospital. It's built on the site of where Fort Whipple once stood.

"See the wooden wall with the stone pillars topped by old-fashioned lamps? Those huge, metal gates between the pillars were found in the weeds, and a group of people took on the project of restoring and reattaching them to the pillars. There was a special ceremony held to re-dedicate the gates and mark the 130th anniversary of the fort."

"Fort Whipple," Dakota said, his voice harsh. "Stop the car, Kathy."

Kathy snapped her head around to look at him, and her breath caught as she saw the tight set to his jaw, the pulse beating in his temple, the fury radiating from his narrowed eyes.

"Dakota, what . . ."

"Stop the car!"

She glanced quickly in the rearview mirror, then eased off the road, driving down a narrow road to park at the gates. She turned off the ignition, then had to hurry to unfasten her seat belt, as Dakota was already out of the car. She caught up with him at the gates, seeing the ramrod stiffness of his body.

"Dakota," she said, "what's wrong? Why are you so upset?"

"I've never seen this fort, but I've known of it for many years," he said, a rough edge to his voice. "Word reached my people where we lived in the Chiricahua Mountains that General Carlton of the Santa Fe soldiers had issued General Order Number 27, which stated that Fort Whipple should be built.

"Through these gates, soldiers rode out time and again to massacre the Apache and Yavapai Indians. These are gates of death, Kathy. *Gates of death.*

"The Apaches who lived up here were not of my tribe, not Chiricahua. They killed many white men who came here after gold was discovered in the Bradshaw Mountains. The Yavapai suffered the consequences of the Apache's actions, and were sent to the San Carlos reservation a few years ago."

He shook his head as though to clear it.

"No, not a few years go. I'm not in my own time." He paused. "Fort Whipple. I hate the very sight of those gates."

"Oh, Dakota, I'm so sorry," Kathy said, her voice trembling with unshed tears. "I never would have mentioned it if I... It's history to me, something that happened so long ago. I didn't mean to cause you this pain, I swear I didn't. I'm so, so sorry." The tears spilled onto her cheeks.

"It's strange to stand here," Dakota said, glancing around, "and realize the soldiers won't appear, prepared to kill me because I'm not of their blood.

"My people wished only to live as we always had, Kathy. The white men came to *our* land, took *our* game to feed themselves, leaving us hungry. They pushed us away like worthless insects who annoyed them. All that was ours, they claimed as their own. What choice did we have but to push back, fight to protect the only way of life we had ever known?"

"Please, Dakota, let's leave here. I apologize for... Oh, God, how could I have been so insensitive, so thoughtless? What is history to me, is your reality. You trusted me and what did I do? I can see the pain in your eyes, on your face."

She dashed tears from her cheeks and struggled to stop crying.

"Different cultures, different worlds," she said, a sob catching in her throat. "This is a perfect example of that. You consider me your wife? Someone who has hurt you like this, just blissfully announced that nifty Fort Whipple was right up ahead? I won't ask you to forgive me, Dakota, because how could you?"

"It's all right," he said, then sighed wearily.

"No, it's not. I feel as though I betrayed your trust in me. The thing is, I'm liable to do it again and again because I forget you're not of this time. You've adapted to this era so wonderfully. You're open and receptive to all the new things you've had to deal with. So what do I do?" She shook her head. "I make certain you don't miss seeing good old Fort Whipple."

"I know you didn't purposely cause me this inner pain, Kathy."

"There's no excuse for what I did. I've started taking your existence here for granted, the way you've adjusted as a given. I've got to remember how different we are, how far apart our worlds are. *I can't forget that.*

"You wanted to hear the list of differences between us?"

She swept one arm through the air. "There's one of the things, Dakota. Those gates, and my lack of sensitivity to who you are, really are. Your wife is supposed to be your best friend. Well, friends don't cause each other pain. They don't."

She moved around him and ran toward the car.

Dakota stood statue-still, staring at the gates, then drew a deep, steadying breath.

There were no soldiers beyond those gates, he told himself. They were not suddenly going to appear and attempt to kill him. He was safe here in Kathy's world.

He turned and started slowly toward the car.

Kathy was being very hard on herself for having mentioned the existence of Fort Whipple, he mused. He could forgive her easily, because he knew in his heart she hadn't intentionally caused him pain. But she knew that, too. She knew it had been an innocent mistake, a momentary lack of judgment on her part.

But...

It was as though she was gathering the incident around her, using it as a shield between them. She was now insisting that it was a perfect example of how different their worlds were, a concrete reason why they couldn't have a future together if they found a way for his spirit to be brought forward in time.

Why was she doing that?

What was she afraid of?

Nine

During the next day and on into Saturday, tension began to build in Kathy and Dakota as the meeting with Dr. Tucker drew near.

Dakota turned his emotions inward and spent more time than usual in the herb garden. He sat cross-legged on the ground, his hands draped loosely over his knees. His back was ramrod-stiff and he appeared to be hardly breathing.

Kathy handled her increasingly frazzled nerves in an opposite manner. She slammed cupboard doors, polished the furniture with a vengeance and muttered a great deal.

After lunch on Saturday, she indulged in a leisurely bubble bath with the hope that the lazy soak in the fragrant, warm water would be soothing. It wasn't. With a cluck of disgust she got out of the tub and began to dry herself with a fluffy towel.

Good grief, she was a wreck. What a helpless, frustrating, vulnerable feeling it was to acknowledge that her entire future rested in the hands of a stranger, a faceless man known to her only as Dr. Tucker.

Kathy hung up the towel, then stilled, staring into space.

This was how Dakota and his people must have felt when the settlers, then later the soldiers, invaded their land. The Indians were at the mercy of others. They no longer had a voice in how and where they would live, or what the future held.

Kathy began to dress slowly, her mind focused on the past, on what she had read in history books.

How incredibly sad it all was, she mused. The white settlers had gathered their courage and come to a harsh new land, searching for better lives and the fulfillment of their dreams for a prosperous future. They had come with hope in their hearts, not hate.

But mistakes born of ignorance had been made. They had moved onto land already claimed by native Americans long before. Fear, then anger, resulted in atrocities being committed by both groups of people. Lives had been lost and dreams destroyed.

Dakota had suffered such tremendous losses, she thought as she left the bathroom. Yet he hadn't hardened his heart to the point of being unable to care deeply for her. He didn't blame her for what had happened, despite her being a descendent of the people who had driven him from his land.

Kathy's mind began to drift toward the memories of the incident with Dakota at the gates of Fort Whipple.

No, she told herself, she wouldn't relive it, not again. It was haunting her. It had become a nightmare that plagued her during the day, as well as in her dreams at night.

After she and Dakota had gotten home that night they had not discussed what had happened at the historic gates. But she couldn't forget it, nor forgive herself for what she'd done.

There was nowhere to escape from the fact that it had been a glaring, painful example of the differences in her and Dakota's worlds.

In the bedroom, Kathy found one tennis shoe, but the other eluded her. She dropped to her knees and peered under the bed.

"Dear heaven," she whispered, then scrambled to her feet. "Dakota!" she yelled.

He appeared a moment later, wearing the blue western shirt, jeans, and a frown.

"Why are you shrieking?" he said.

"The Dream Catcher," she said, her voice trembling.

"What about it?"

"Oh, Dakota, it's not as big as it was." She dropped to her knees again and slid the Dream Catcher carefully from beneath the bed. "See?"

Dakota hunkered down, balancing on the balls of his feet. His frown deepened.

"It was easily six feet across the morning you came here," Kathy said, "but now it's... I don't know for sure, but it appears to be less than five feet in width."

Dakota nodded slowly.

Kathy clutched one of his arms with both hands.

"What does this mean?" she said, a frantic edge to her voice.

"I'm not certain, and I can only guess. I think the powers of the Dream Catcher that were in full force when I was transported here are now diminishing. Why? I don't know.''

He looked at Kathy.

''We're fighting the enemy of time twofold now, Kathy. I must be united with my center spirit before it's too late and I die. And, the mystery of the Dream Catcher must be solved before its remaining powers are gone. I don't hold much hope in my heart for a victory.''

''Yes, you do,'' she said, tightening her grip on his arm. ''You *won't* give up, Dakota. Do you hear me? We don't know what Dr. Tucker is going to tell us, but I sense that we'll need to be strong, to believe in what he says, to enable us to do our part.''

''And if he has no answers?''

''He will, Dakota. *He will.* Come on, let's go. We have to meet Lily and Brad. Oh, blast, where's my stupid shoe?''

As they drove to Lily and Brad's, Kathy chattered on about Territorial Days, unable to bear the tension-laden silence in the car.

Held every year, she related, Territorial Days were very popular with Prescott residents, as well as the multitude of tourists who drove up the mountain to attend.

The main event was held a block from the town square on the grounds of the Sharlot Hall Museum complex.

One of the buildings besides the intriguing museum was the original residence, built back in 1864, of the Territorial Governor, John Goodwin, and the Secretary of the Territory, Richard McCormick.

Another structure built in 1864 had been a general store that later belonged to Judge John Howard, who sentenced frontier criminals for their offenses. Since the judge dispensed "misery" to the miscreants, the little house was called Fort Misery.

Kathy rambled on about the other buildings, some of which had been carefully moved onto the site to preserve them for future generations.

"You'll see people in costumes depicting the times when the buildings were actually in use," she said. "Women will be dipping candles, operating spinning wheels, cowboys will make biscuits over a campfire, all kinds of things. It's fun."

"Mmm" was all Dakota had to say about Kathy's dissertation.

At Lily and Brad's, Lily said she didn't have the energy to go with them.

"It's so crowded, and I'm having an 'I'm totally exhausted so don't mess with me' day. I'll stay home with the girls. You find Dr. Tucker and his wife and bring them here for lemonade and cookies. You can't have a serious discussion in the mob down there."

"I could wait here with you, Lily," Kathy said.

"No, no, you'll be a nervous wreck and you'll drive me nuts. You go on with Brad and Dakota. Shoo. You don't want to be late meeting Dr. Tucker, and finding a place to park will be a good trick." She flapped her hands at them. "Goodbye, goodbye."

As the trio trudged the last block to the Sharlot Hall complex, Brad chuckled.

"We should have walked from the house," he said, "considering how far away we had to park. We're meeting Dr. Tucker and his wife at the front entrance of the museum. They were planning on coming over early to have time to enjoy all the Territorial Days doings, so they'll be ready to leave with us."

Kathy slipped her hand into Dakota's and held fast.

"Let's cut across here," Brad said. "We'll be in the middle of the crowd, but Dakota will be able to see some of what's going on. It's very unique, very clever and authentic. These folks really give it their all. You'll feel as though you've already been transported back in time, Dakota."

"Mmm," he said.

As they stepped off the sidewalk onto the lawn, they were immediately caught up in the crunch of people. Dakota's fingers tightened around Kathy's.

There were too many people, his mind hammered. They were surrounding him, pressing in from every direction. He'd never been in a place where so many were gathered. It was too loud, too confining.

"Dakota?" Kathy said as they maneuvered their way slowly forward. "Are you all right?"

"I can't breathe here, Kathy," he said, beads of sweat dotting his brow.

"Ah, damn," Brad said, "where was my mind? I'm sorry, Dakota, I just didn't think. I don't imagine you've ever been in a crowd like this one."

"No."

"I'm to blame," Kathy said miserably. "I can't believe I did this to you again, Dakota. Bringing you here was as thoughtless and insensitive as my showing you the gates of Fort Whipple." She shook her head in self-disgust. "I'm hopeless. I can't seem to handle the differences between our worlds at all. I continually cause you pain and..."

"Kathy," Brad interrupted, "I don't know what happened at Fort Whipple, but let's not stand around discussing it. We have to get Dakota out of this crowd."

"Yes, of course," she said. "I'm sorry. Oh, dear, I continually do things that I have to apologize for. I *am* sorry, Dakota."

"Come on," Brad said. "Keep moving as quickly as possible. If we can get through this section, we'll be at the sidewalk leading to the museum."

Dakota nodded, but his eyes continued to dart back and forth. The wild tempo of his heart echoed in his ears.

His urge to run, to flee to safety, was nearly overwhelming, requiring every ounce of willpower he possessed to continue to place one foot in front of the other.

Remain calm, he ordered himself. He must stay calm, reach deep within himself for courage. He was in no danger there. There were too many people, *too many*, but they were friendly. They were not his enemies. They weren't hunting for him, they weren't even paying any attention to him. He could see the walkway up ahead. Calm. *Remain calm.*

Suddenly Dakota halted dead in his tracks, every muscle in his body tensing. Kathy turned her head to see what Dakota was staring at beyond her.

"Oh, dear heaven," she whispered.

Ambling toward them were two men dressed in the blue uniforms of frontier cavalry soldiers and carrying old-fashioned rifles.

"Run, Kathy," Dakota said, his voice rough. "Go. Your safety comes first. I'll delay the soldiers while you find a place to hide. Go. Now."

She moved quickly in front of him and gripped his arms.

"Dakota, listen to me," she said, a frantic edge to her voice. "Those men are not really soldiers. They dressed in those uniforms to be part of Territorial Days. It's all pretend, Dakota. It's not real."

"Run!" he yelled.

Several people turned to look at him curiously.

"Dakota..." Brad said.

"Please, listen to me, Dakota," Kathy said. *"Look at me."*

He slowly shifted his gaze from the still-advancing soldiers to look directly into her eyes.

"You consider me your woman," she said softly, "your wife. I know I've made terrible mistakes, caused you much upset, but I'm asking you to trust me one more time, believe in me. No one is going to hurt you. Those soldiers aren't real. They're no threat to you. *Hear me."*

Dakota stared at her for another long moment, then drew a shuddering breath that rippled through his body. His shoulders slumped as the tension ebbed from his muscles, then he squared his shoulders again.

"I hear you, Kathy," he said, a gritty quality to his voice.

The soldiers strolled past them.

"Howdy, folks," one of them said. "Enjoying yourselves?"

Brad let out a pent-up breath. "Oh, yes," he said dryly, "we're having a terrific time."

"Way to go," the soldier said.

"I'm such a lamebrain," Brad muttered.

"Are you all right now, Dakota?" Kathy said.

"Mmm," he said, nodding.

"You put my safety first," she said, a ring of awe in her voice. "You told me to run and hide while you fought off the soldiers."

"I'm an Apache brave of honor. I protect my woman from harm at any cost. That's how it's meant to be."

"Fancy that," she said, managing to produce a small smile. "If I were you, I wouldn't even speak to me, let alone protect me."

"Let's hurry up," Brad said.

They left the lawn and started along the sidewalk toward the museum.

Dr. and Mrs. Tucker, Kathy decided, looked exactly as a retired professor and his wife should.

John Tucker was short and round with thick gray hair and wire-rimmed glasses. He had a smile that caused crinkling lines to form by his eyes, and there was a warm and friendly aura emanating from him. He introduced his wife, Evelyn, who was a carbon copy of him in female form.

"You have no idea how much of a pleasure this is, Dakota," Dr. Tucker said, shaking Dakota's hand. "I've been counting the hours until I could meet you." He released Dakota's hand and glanced around. "I wouldn't have thought you'd be comfortable in this atmosphere."

"There are wise men," Brad said, "and there are dumb men. Color me dumb."

"Well, let's leave, shall we?" Evelyn said. "I'm sure Dakota has had quite enough of Territorial Days."

Brad gave Dr. Tucker directions to the house, saying they would rendezvous there.

Twenty minutes later, they were all settled in Lily and Brad's living room, sipping lemonade.

"Dr. Tucker," Kathy said, "before you tell us if you've discovered anything that will help us, I want to say that it's our fervent hope that Dakota's center spirit can be transported here, rather than sending him back to 1877. There's nothing left for him in his own time. It's gone, everything he had, the existence he knew. He wants to stay *here*."

Dr. Tucker looked at Kathy, then at Dakota, back at Kathy, and nodded.

"Am I assuming too much," he said, "to believe you are now married by Apache custom?"

"Kathy is my wife," Dakota said.

"Oh, well, I . . ." Kathy said, feeling the heat of embarrassment on her cheeks. She threw up her hands in defeat.

"Oh, bless your hearts," Evelyn Tucker said.

Brad leaned forward in his chair, rested his elbows on his knees, and made a steeple of his fingers.

"What have you discovered since we talked on the phone, Dr. Tucker?" he said. "Have you solved the mystery of the Dream Catcher?"

Please, Kathy begged silently. *Say yes. Dr. Tucker, please, say yes.*

"No," the professor said, frowning.

"Oh, God," Kathy whispered, then pressed trembling fingertips to her lips.

"Now wait," Dr. Tucker said, raising both hands. "*I* don't have the answer, but after talking to a multitude of native Americans I know in Flagstaff, I've gathered information that *might* be the solution. There's no guarantee about this. I want you to fully realize that."

"We'll try anything," Kathy said. "Dakota will die if he isn't united with the center of his spirit."

"Yes, my dear," John Tucker said, "he will. I was told that more than once during my interviews. Time is of the utmost importance."

"There's something you don't know," Kathy said. "We haven't even told Lily and Brad yet because we found out just as we were leaving the house."

"What?" Lily said. "What is it?"

"The Dream Catcher," Dakota said quietly, "is becoming smaller. It's less than five feet across now."

"Why?" Lily said, her voice rising. "What does that mean?"

"Let me tell you what I've managed to find out," Dr. Tucker said. "First of all, it might surprise you to learn that none of the native Americans I spoke with had any doubt that someone could be transported through time with a Dream Catcher."

"John presented it hypothetically, of course," Evelyn said. "No one he interviewed even suspected that he was dealing with an actual situation."

"Correct," John said. "An old gentleman told me that it's very common for two people who are meant to be together, soul mates, if you will, to be kept apart by time, by where they exist in history, due to a subtle shift in the moon when they were born.

"That, the old gentleman said, is why there is so much unhappiness in the world, such discord in marriages. The person they were meant to be with is in another era, never to be known to them."

Kathy blinked. "What? Are you saying..." Her voice trailed off as she stared at Dr. Tucker.

"Yes, dear," Evelyn said, smiling, "you and Dakota are soul mates, you belong together."

"It's very complex," John said. "Three things have to be in perfect synchronization. The people must be thinking at exactly the same moment about what is missing from their lives. They must be wishing to feel complete. Obviously you two were doing that.

"The third ingredient is to have the means to unite those people." He lifted both hands palms up. "The Dream Catcher."

"My stars," Lily said, "isn't that something? Kathy and Dakota are soul mates, are each other's ... destiny. Yes, that's an excellent word."

Dakota crossed his arms over his chest and nodded. "So be it."

"Now, wait a minute," Kathy said. "Just hold it here."

"Yes, dear?" Evelyn said. "What do you wish to say, Kathy?"

"Well..." Kathy shook her head. "I have no idea. It's too much to comprehend, to believe."

"*I* believe it," Dakota said.

"Dr. Tucker," Brad said, "if all this is true, then why didn't Dakota's spirit travel with him through time?"

"Because a part of him was still holding on to life as he'd known it before he was longing for what was now missing. He was emotionally struggling against the reality of his present existence."

"Oh, darn," Lily said, "that makes sense, it really does."

"Why is the Dream Catcher shrinking?" Kathy said, a rather frantic edge to her voice.

Dr. Tucker sighed. "I was told about such a thing happening, but didn't know it applied here until now. The diminishing in size of the Dream Catcher means that one of the pair is fighting against what has taken place, what has happened. For reasons known only to them, they aren't accepting the other person's role in their life. That is draining the Dream Catcher of its power."

"All right, you guys," Lily said, glaring at Kathy and Dakota, "which one of you is gumming up the works?"

"My darling wife," Brad said, chuckling, "that is none of your business."

"Oh," Lily said. "Well, what if said unknown person gets their act together...quickly. Will the Dream Catcher stop shrinking?"

"I really don't know," Dr. Tucker said. "No one I spoke with knew how to stop the shrinking, only what was causing it. To be safe, we'll have to proceed assuming the Dream Catcher will continue to decrease in size."

"Mmm," Dakota said, frowning.

"We're now facing two races against time," Dr. Tucker continued. "We must accomplish our goals before the remaining spirit within Dakota is depleted, and before the Dream Catcher becomes nothing more than the small ornament it was when Kathy originally bought it."

"What are we to do?" Kathy said, clutching her hands tightly in her lap. "Dr. Tucker?"

"There is, supposedly," he said, "an old shaman living down in the Chiricahua Mountains. I say 'supposedly' because no one I spoke to has actually seen him, nor knows anyone who has. The majority had heard of him, though. He's believed to be very powerful, a true shaman. The consensus was that if anyone could control the Dream Catcher's magic, it would be that shaman."

Dakota nodded.

"You must take the Dream Catcher," Dr. Tucker said, "go down to the southern part of the state to the Chiricahua Mountains, and find that shaman."

"As quickly as possible," Evelyn interjected.

"Indeed," John said, patting her knee. "I'll draw you a map of the general area in the Chiricahua Mountains where the shaman has been rumored to have been seen."

"I know the Chiricahuas," Dakota said. "I'm a Chiricahua Apache. Those mountains are...were...my home."

"Dr. Tucker," Lily said, her voice unsteady, "we don't want to lose Dakota, none of us do. This baby—" she rested her hands on her stomach "—is to be named Michelle Dakota Benson."

"I'm honored to have your child hold my name," Dakota said.

Kathy pressed her fingertips to her aching temples. "I feel so overwhelmed. It's too much to take in. I need time to sort through all of this."

"If there's one thing we're short of, it's time," Brad said. "Dr. Tucker, in your honest opinion, sir, what do you think the chances are of Dakota surviving this?"

"I don't know, son," he said quietly. "I just don't know."

Ten

To Kathy's relief, the remainder of the afternoon and on into the evening was filled with activities that would make it possible for her to leave town for an undetermined length of time.

When she telephoned Sally to inquire if she would be available to run The Herb Hogan, her assistant immediately assumed that Kathy and Dakota were finally going on their honeymoon.

"Yes," Kathy said quickly, pointing one finger in the air. "That's it, that's exactly what we're doing. A honeymoon trip. Good idea. What I mean is, aren't you the clever one to have figured that out? There's no keeping a secret from you, Sally."

"Ha! You've tried to keep the secret of your marriage to Dakota from everyone, you sneaky person, with you saying you weren't his wife and him declaring you were. You're so silly sometimes, Kathy. Anyway, I hope you have a fabulous honeymoon. Stay away as long as you like and don't worry about the store.''

"Well, Dakota and I will take more herbs to the store later today. There are shipments due in from Flagstaff and Sedona, so you'll be all set. I have a neighbor boy coming to water my garden. I just don't know for certain when we'll be back.''

Nor did she know if she'd be returning to Prescott alone, she thought dismally. No, no, she wouldn't dwell on that now.

"Oh-h-h, this is so romantic," Sally said. "I don't suppose you're telling anyone where you're going."

"No."

"I don't blame you. You and Dakota want to be alone, just the two of you."

And an old shaman, Kathy mused, who held the key, the only hope, for saving Dakota's life.

"Yes, just the two of us," Kathy said quietly. "Thanks a million, Sally. It's wonderful to be able to go away and know the store is receiving your tender loving care. You're a wonderful friend."

"It's my pleasure. Enjoy your trip. Bye for now, Kathy."

Kathy and Dakota stocked The Herb Hogan to overflowing, then stopped to purchase two more shirts for Dakota, plus travel-size personal items. Back at the house they ate dinner, managing to keep the conversation light, then Kathy packed a small suitcase, leaving out last-minute things they'd use in the morning.

As darkness fell, Kathy spread out a map of Arizona on the kitchen table.

"Okay, let's see," she said. "We're here. It's about a two-hour drive to Phoenix, another two to Tucson, and two more to Douglas, down on the Mexican border. If we stay overnight in Douglas, we can start out fresh for the Chiricahua Mountains on Monday morning. Does that sound all right to you, Dakota?''

She turned to look at him where he stood next to her by the table.

"Yes," he said, nodding. "Your plan is..." Suddenly he grabbed the back of a chair as he pressed his other hand to his forehead. "I... The room moves... I..."

"Dakota?" Kathy said, flinging her arms around his chest. "Are you in pain? Are you dizzy? What is it? Talk to me."

"I have to sit down," he said, sinking slowly to the floor.

Kathy moved with him, anxiously watching his face. He closed his eyes, shook his head slightly, and drew a deep breath. He opened his eyes again tentatively.

"The room has stopped spinning," he said. "I feel stronger now. For a moment I was very weak. I didn't have the strength to stand. This was much worse than the other time I felt strange."

"Dear heaven," Kathy said, her eyes widened in horror, "then it's happening faster, isn't it. Your spirit is flowing out of your body and can't be replaced because the center isn't there."

"Yes." He stroked her cheek gently with his thumb. "I'm sorry."

She encircled his neck with her arms and nestled her head on his chest.

"*You're* sorry?" she said, her eyes filling with tears. "I've spent the day doing everything but facing the truth of what Dr. Tucker said."

"My center spirit didn't travel with me through the Dream Catcher because I was still clinging to my existence in the past."

"That's true, but you know that is not what I'm talking about. The Dream Catcher is shrinking because one of us hasn't acknowledged the other's role in their life. That's me, Dakota, and we're both aware of that fact. You consider me your wife, but I won't accept the title because..."

"You don't love me," he interrupted quietly. "That's not your fault. You can't force emotions upon yourself, they have to just come. Just be there."

A sob caught in Kathy's throat. "But I care so deeply for you. I want you to stay here with me more than I can even begin to tell you. There's so much for me to deal with, Dakota, and it's all confusing and frightening. What if I really do love you, but I'm such a muddled mess I don't realize I do? Oh-h-h, I can't stand this."

"Don't cry," he said, stroking her back in a soothing motion. "I have sensed your fear of loving me, Kathy. What are you afraid of?"

"We haven't had enough time together to make discoveries. We're from different worlds, different cultures. Twice now I've caused you pain by being thoughtless and insensitive because I forgot you were from another time. *Forgot*."

"Did it ever occur to you that you've accepted me so completely into your life that it's a natural and wonderful thing that you forget that I arrived here from another era? Ah, Kathy, are we really all that different? We're man and woman, united, one. With the concept of compromise you've taught me, I truly believe we can mesh our worlds *if* we want to badly enough."

Kathy shifted slightly so she could look directly at him.

"Well," she said, tears echoing in her voice, "I *did* think about the fact that you could be my partner at The Herb Hogan if you wanted to. You know all about herbs, their uses, how to grow and dry them. We might even be able to open a second store in Prescott Valley or Chino Valley, the next towns over."

Dakota nodded. "That plan has great value."

"But... Oh, Dakota, to marry? To make a commitment to forever? It's so risky, so dangerous, because we've had so little time together. I..." She shook her head as a sob caught in her throat.

"I understand. I can't fight your demons of fear for you, Kathy. They are yours, within you, and there's nothing I can do, despite my skills as an Apache brave. That battle is yours... alone."

"I'm so sorry, Dakota," she said, crying openly. "*I'm* causing the Dream Catcher to shrink. It's *my* fault. You must be so hurt because of that, so angry at me. You must be close to hating me."

"No, Kathy," he said, "I'm not close to hating you at all. I love you, Kathy Maxwell. My caring for you enough to name you my wife has grown. I love you."

Kathy dashed the tears from her cheeks, then took a trembling breath.

"You...you love me?" she said. "You're *in* love with me?"

Dakota nodded.

"Oh, dear, I don't know if that's wonderful, or terrible. I'm so confused, so..."

"Hush," he said, then brushed his lips over hers. "There's no purpose to be served by discussing this further now. We've both been open and honest with each other about our feelings.''

''And they don't match, don't mesh.''

''So be it.''

''Oh, Dakota, I'm sorry, so sorry.''

''Let's get off the floor. Do you know that when I first came here I thought you'd grown this carpet in here? I've learned a great deal. Perhaps you should give thought to what *you've* learned.'' He released her and rolled to his feet.

Kathy scrambled up next to him. ''Do you feel strong enough to stand?''

''I'm fine now. I don't know how this will progress, Kathy. I've only seen it happen once before many years ago, and it may differ from person to person. What *is* clear, is that we're running out of time very quickly.''

''Yes,'' she said softly, ''I know. Well, we'll go to bed now, get a solid night's sleep, then start out fresh at dawn tomorrow. Dakota, we have to believe that we'll find the shaman in time and he'll have the answer we need. *We have to believe that.*''

Dakota nodded, then encircled her with his arms and captured her mouth in a searing kiss. They went to bed and made slow, sweet love, going together to the place that held the beautiful wildflowers.

Just before Kathy fell into a restless sleep, Dakota's words echoed in her mind.

Perhaps you should give thought to what you've learned.

They awoke at dawn to the sound of a soft, steady rain. While Kathy usually enjoyed a rainy day as much as one brilliant with sunlight, the weather seemed a dark omen that heightened her fears.

They spoke little as they ate breakfast, cleaned the kitchen, then loaded the car.

"Well, it's time to collect the Dream Catcher," Kathy said finally, failing to produce a lightness to her voice that she'd been striving for.

"I'll get it," Dakota said.

As he walked away, Kathy closed her eyes and took a steadying breath.

She had to gain control, she told herself. She felt as though she was falling apart by inches. Her world, the very essence of who she was, was chipping away, piece by piece. There were hours of driving to be done, then a trek into the Chiricahua Mountains. She had to be strong, not only in body, but in mind, as well.

What she would *not* dwell on was that Dakota loved her. *Loved her.* That fact, combined with her muddled emotions, was too much to deal with now, just too much.

"Kathy," Dakota said, bringing her from her tormented thoughts.

She looked up and a gasp escaped from her lips.

Dakota was holding the Dream Catcher.

And it was no more than three feet wide.

"Oh, dear heaven, Dakota," she said, her voice trembling.

"Well, it will fit easily in the back seat of your metal egg known as the car," he said.

"Oh, Dakota," she said, managing a small smile, "you'd find the bright side of the bleakest day." The Dream Catcher was getting smaller and smaller, and it was her fault! "Are you ready to go?"

He came to the middle of the living room and glanced around, his gaze touching each piece of furniture in turn.

"This is my home now," he said quietly. "I want to return here, to live out my days and nights with you." He looked at Kathy. "Let's get started on our journey. We have a long way to go."

"And a shaman to find."

"Mmm," he said, nodding.

The rain continued to fall as they drove down the mountain toward the valley below that held the huge city of Phoenix. As Kathy came to each section of the road that was comprised of twisting, turning curves, she directed her full attention to driving.

Approaching Phoenix, the rain lessened, then stopped. The number of cars on the road increased, and they were soon caught up in bumper-to-bumper traffic. She glanced quickly at Dakota and saw the deep frown on his face.

"I know it's crowded," she said, "but we're going around the edge of the city on this highway. We'll be back in open country soon, and you'll be able to see all the way to the horizon during the drive to Tucson. We'll stop at a rest station on the far side of Phoenix and stretch our legs. Would you like to listen to some music?"

"Mmm," Dakota said.

Kathy tuned the radio to a country western station and began to hum along with a familiar song. A few minutes later she realized Dakota was scowling at the radio.

"What's a 'thang'?" he said.

"A who?" Kathy said. "Oh, he's saying 'thing.' The words of the song are 'love is a wonderful thing.'"

"No, he said, 'Love is a wonderful thang.'"

"Yes, I know, but..." She pressed a button on the panel. "Let's go for easy-listening music. Explaining country western to you would exhaust me. If they played 'Achy Breaky Heart,' you'd be totally confused.''

After they left the rest station, Dakota sighed and leaned his head back on the top of the seat.

"Dakota?" Kathy said. "Is something wrong?"

"I need to rest."

"Are you having another attack of weakness?"

"Mmm. I'll sleep now, Kathy."

"Yes," she said, her hands tightening on the steering wheel. "Yes, good, that's good. Rest, sleep, so you can regain your strength."

She pressed harder on the gas pedal.

Hurry, her mind screamed. They were going too slow, using up too much precious time getting to the Chiricahua Mountains. Dakota's spirit was flowing from his body, the Dream Catcher was shrinking in size and... *Hurry*.

She shook her head in self-disgust and eased up on the pedal.

Getting a speeding ticket wasn't the solution, she admonished herself. They were doing the best they could, covering the maddening distance one mile at a time. But would their best be enough to save Dakota's life?

It had to be. It just had to be. Please!

By the time they reached the border town of Douglas, darkness had fallen and Kathy was thoroughly fatigued from the long drive.

Dakota had awakened from an hour's nap to assure her that he was once again feeling fine. They'd chatted on and off about rather mundane topics, but always there was the ever-building tension born of the knowledge of why they were making the trip.

They ate dinner at a small café, then checked into a motel, placing the Dream Catcher carefully on top of a table that sat in the corner of the room. Kathy was asleep within moments of her head touching the pillow.

Dakota stared up at a ceiling he couldn't see in the darkness, the fingers of one hand entwined with Kathy's. He sighed, feeling as though he was being crushed by the weight of his despair.

Kathy, his mind whispered. His woman. His wife. He loved her, honored and respected her, wished for her to bear his son, the many children, of his seed.

But he was dying.

He'd been overcome with the weakness again while Kathy had been in the shower. He'd managed to remove his clothes and get into bed before she came out of the bathroom. His spirit was leaving his body more quickly now, and there was nothing he could do to stop it.

Nothing.

As an Apache brave he wasn't afraid of death, of going to his eternal beyond. No, it wasn't fear that consumed him, it was sorrow. He didn't want to leave Kathy. He wanted to stay with her for all time.

He had only himself to blame for the fact that his spirit was flowing from him. At the moment Kathy's yearnings for a soul mate had intertwined with his through the Dream Catcher, he'd been clinging to the past, to what he'd once been, the way of life that had brought him happiness, fulfillment and inner peace.

Like a child holding stubbornly to a toy that wasn't his, a small portion of his mind had been refusing to let go of all he had ever known.

Because of his foolishness, his spirit had been left behind when the Dream Catcher flung him forward in time to be united with Kathy.

But the shrinking of the Dream Catcher?

It was diminishing in size because Kathy Maxwell had declared that she didn't love him as he loved her. And that hurt. It caused an ache in his heart beyond measure.

They needed more time to make discoveries, she'd said. To determine if the differences in their worlds could be overcome by compromise. She cared deeply for him, but she wasn't in love with him.

She was telling the truth as she knew it. She would never lie to him, but he was certain she wasn't being honest with herself. Her true feelings for him were buried beneath the fear of loving, of making a commitment to forever.

And there wasn't anything he could do about it.

Dakota's free hand curled into a tight fist of anger and frustration. He felt like a helpless infant, unable to gain control over his own destiny.

In his era, he'd been dictated to by the soldiers who hunted him with the intention of killing him.

Now?

He was held in the web of the mysteries of the Dream Catcher, and had been rendered completely vulnerable.

The Dream Catcher had worked its magic and brought Kathy and him together in the place where they both belonged. But their human frailties were destroying the gifts of the Dream Catcher, which were offered to very few.

Their only hope was the shaman. A true shaman was filled with wisdom beyond common man. Perhaps *his* powers would be stronger than the weaknesses of Kathy Maxwell and Dakota Smith.

They had to find that shaman!

Dakota finally slept, but he was restless, tossing and turning through the long, dark hours of the night.

When Kathy and Dakota awoke the next morning, the Dream Catcher was only two feet wide.

Eleven

It had rained during the night, and the day was hot and humid. Kathy reaffirmed in her mind that she definitely preferred living in mile-high Prescott, with its clear, cool air.

For breakfast they went to the same café where they'd eaten dinner the night before. While they ate, Kathy studied the map that Dr. Tucker had drawn for them. When the friendly waitress returned to the table to refill their coffee cups, Kathy smiled at her.

"Excuse me," Kathy said, "but I was wondering if you've ever heard of anyone seeing the old shaman who reportedly lives in the Chiricahua Mountains?"

The waitress stilled the coffeepot in midair and planted her other hand on an ample hip.

"Well, I've sure heard tell of him," she said. "There's been rumors of that old guy for years. Folks have come down here for the sole purpose of finding him, but no one ever has, as far as I know. I think it's just a wives' tale that there's an Indian medicine man in those mountains. Nope, I don't believe he exists, I truly don't."

She looked at Dakota.

"Is he supposed to be a relative of yours or something, sugar?"

Dakota shook his head.

"We need to find him," Kathy said. Her eyes widened as she realized the waitress had actually batted her eyelashes at Dakota. "It's very important."

"Well, good luck to you," the waitress said. She slid a glance at Dakota. "Is there anything else you want? For breakfast?"

"No," Kathy said, unable to stifle a burst of laughter. "Thank you."

"You bet," the woman said, then sashayed away.

"You have just been flirted with, Mr. Smith," Kathy said, smiling.

Dakota frowned. "If she doesn't change her ways, she'll end up with her nose split."

"Oh, good heavens, don't get started on that gruesome stuff." She paused, all traces of her smile gone. "Are you feeling all right this morning?"

"I'm fine."

"That's good. Well, according to this map, it will take more than an hour to drive to the mountains and as far in as we can go by car. We'll have to walk the rest of the way to where Dr. Tucker's friends said the shaman lives."

"Mmm," Dakota said, nodding.

Kathy leaned forward and covered one of his hands with hers on the top of the table.

"Dakota, you must promise me you'll stop and rest whenever you need to. It's hot and humid, and Dr.

Tucker said the Chiricahuas are rough-going in places. Don't be all macho and tough. Tell me when you need a break. Okay?''

"It's not difficult to move through the Chiricahuas. I've done it my entire life."

"Oh, that's right. You live...lived...there. Well, I'd still appreciate it if you'd promise me you won't push yourself. Please?"

"I hear you, Kathy. Let's go. We're wasting time." He paused. "I love you, Kathy. We will find the shaman, and he'll know the answer to the mystery of the Dream Catcher. Everything is going to be fine."

They looked at each other for a long moment, each desperately wanting to believe what he had said, each knowing it might not be true.

"Come," he said finally, getting to his feet.

Kathy tried to enjoy the beauty of the area through which they drove, but with every passing mile she grew more tense, her breakfast sitting like a heavy stone in the pit of her stomach.

The going was slow for the last several miles as she inched the car over a dirt road that was an obstacle course of deep ruts. The road ended in a grove of tall trees and enormous rocks.

"Well, this is the end of the trail," she said, turning off the ignition.

"The Chiricahuas," Dakota said, his gaze sweeping over the area. "I know this land."

After locking the car, Kathy slipped the keys into the pocket of her jeans. They clipped the water-filled sports bottles to their belt loops, then Dakota tucked the Dream Catcher under one arm. Kathy studied the map, looked around, then scrutinized the paper again.

"That way," she said, pointing to the left. "I think."

Dakota stood behind her and looked over her shoulder at the map.

"You have it upside down, Kathy," he said. "If we go to the left, we'll eventually end up back at the paved road we were on."

"Oh," she said, flipping the paper around. "Well, I never claimed to be Daniel Boone."

"Who?"

"Never mind. Let's see here. Okay, we go to the right." She looked in that direction. "How can we do that? There are huge boulders in the way."

"We climb over them."

"You can't be serious. When Dr. Tucker said it was rough-going in places, I didn't realize he meant we were in for actual mountain climbing."

"The rocks aren't going to move out of the path just because you don't want to climb them, Kathy. We'll come to much steeper terrain before we reach the area Dr. Tucker marked on that map."

"Oh, good grief," she said, rolling her eyes heavenward. "This is going to be hard work. I'm not into exercise, Dakota. My idea of a walk is going to my mailbox, or strolling around the town square in Prescott." She sighed. "Well, let's get started. You'd better lead the way. I have a feeling I'd have us thoroughly lost in ten minutes or less."

"Definitely less," he said, starting forward.

"Thanks a lot," she muttered.

"You are welcome."

A little over an hour later, Kathy moaned.

"Dakota," she said, "slow down. No, even better ... stop. I've got to rest."

He halted and turned to look at her.

"Again?" he said, raising his eyebrows. "This is the third time since we started."

She sank onto the ground beneath a tall tree. "Who's counting? Oh-h-h, my legs, my feet, my entire body, are screaming for mercy."

Dakota chuckled and sat beside her.

"You're not even out of breath," she said, glaring at him. "You move up and over those boulders as though they weren't even there. Worse yet, you only have one free hand because you're carrying the Dream Catcher. That's borderline rude, Mr. Smith." She leaned her head against the trunk of the tree and closed her eyes. "Oh-h-h."

"I'm very accustomed to this country, Kathy."

"I'm ethnically disadvantaged," she said, not opening her eyes. "Translated that means I'm a wreck because I'm not an Indian."

"Mmm," Dakota said, nodding. "That conclusion has merit."

Kathy opened her eyes and looked at him.

"Have you had any waves of weakness or dizziness?" she asked.

"No, nothing. In fact, I feel very strong. I wonder..." His gaze swept over the area. "Perhaps I've stopped the flowing out of my spirit for a while by coming to the place of my birth, the place where I was raised and lived. I don't know, but it's possible, I suppose."

Kathy lifted her head from the tree. "That would be wonderful, Dakota. It would mean we have more time to find the shaman." She looked at the Dream Catcher where it lay on Dakota's thighs. "The Dream Catcher isn't any smaller than it was when we left Douglas."

"No."

"We probably should have wrapped it in something. It could snag on a bush or tree and be damaged. I should have thought of that and protected it."

"No, I don't think so," he said slowly. "I believe, although I'm not certain as to why, that it shouldn't be covered. It has great powers, and a true shaman has great powers."

"You mean the shaman might sense that the Dream Catcher is near him? He might pick up some kind of vibes from it, or whatever?"

"Maybe." He looked up at the trees surrounding them. "The trees are much taller now than when I lived here. It's strange to see this."

"Yes, I imagine it is," she said quietly, then paused. "How much farther do we have to go before we reach the area where the shaman is supposed to be? *And* how large of an area do we have to search through?"

"At the speed you travel, it will be a while yet before we're in the section where the shaman is believed to be. That area, though, isn't large because it's surrounded by steep rocks forming a small canyon. He'll either be there, or he won't."

"He'll be there," Kathy said decisively.

"The woman in the café said many others have sought him, Kathy, but no one has found him. They no doubt had the same knowledge we have."

"I don't care. *We* will find him." She got to her feet. "Come on."

They trekked for another hour, Kathy only allowing herself two stops to rest. The terrain was becoming rockier, and Dakota had to reach down and extend his free hand to her time and again to pull her up and over a huge boulder. The trees were thicker, closer together, and the going was frustratingly slow.

As they emerged from an extremely dense group of trees, Dakota suddenly stopped dead in his tracks, causing Kathy to bump into him from behind. She moved to his side to see what had caused his abrupt halt.

She saw a clearing the size of a football field, where no trees grew. There were bushes spotting the area, some wildflowers and clumps of weeds.

"Dakota?" she said, looking up at him questioningly.

"This..." he started, then shook his head. He cleared his throat, took a deep breath, then let it out slowly. "This was where I lived, where my people had their camp. I was born here, grew up here. It was from this place that my people were driven away. They had to leave here when they went to the reservation."

"Oh, Dakota," she whispered, seeing the pain in his eyes, hearing it in his voice.

"I can envision it all," he went on. "Our homes, the children playing, the women working, the fires burning to cook our food. I lived there." He pointed to the right. "Our horses were kept in that area." He swept his hand in another direction. "Meat was smoked over a fire at that far end."

"Dakota..."

"I can hear them. The voices of my people are reaching me, Kathy. The echo of their sorrow is carried on the wind. There is no laughter, only the sound of crying, of deep sadness."

"Oh, Dakota, don't do this to yourself. Let's move on. This is so painful for you."

"I stood in those trees on the other side," he said as though she hadn't spoken, "and watched them leave with the soldiers. My people walked tall, straight. Proud Chiricahua Apaches even in their hour of defeat.

"In a single line they went, not speaking. Even the children were silent. Even the babies made no sound. And as they left, not one of them turned to look back upon what had been theirs, what they would never see again."

A sob caught in Kathy's throat, and she covered her mouth with one hand.

Dakota stood ramrod stiff, staring at the clearing, reliving it all, the memories beating unmercifully against his mind. A shudder ripped through him with such painful intensity it caused him to take a sharp breath.

Thunder rumbled in the distance, snapping him back to the present, causing the past to release him from its cold, tormenting fist.

"It's threatening to rain," he said, his voice still husky with emotion, "and it comes quickly in these mountains. We'll have to take shelter, Kathy, because the lightning that accompanies summer storms is very dangerous among these trees."

"But we'll lose time, Dakota."

"It can't be helped. See how the sky darkens? We only have a few minutes."

"Where will we go?"

"I know a place where the rocks form a type of cave. We'll be safe there." He looked at the sky again, then reached for her hand. "We'll have to run. We'll cross... we'll cross the clearing that was my home, move through those trees beyond, then we'll be a short distance from the cave. Come on, Kathy. Hurry."

They ran.

Dakota had to shorten his stride so Kathy could keep up. The dark clouds rolled across the sky like a wild current in a raging river, roaring with thunder as they came. Lightning streaked through the heavens in jagged, bright slashes, then large drops of rain began to fall.

They ran across the field of memories into the woods beyond, then emerged on the other side to find huge boulders in their path. Dakota veered to the right, then upward over the rocks, still holding tightly to Kathy's hand. The rain increased, soaking them to the skin and drenching the Dream Catcher.

It was becoming darker, like dusk inching toward night, and the noise was deafening. The thunder rumbled, the lightning crackled, wind whipped the trees into a frenzy and seemed to moan like the voices of a multitude of ghosts as it tunneled through the crevices between the rocks.

Kathy's heart pounded, not only from physical exertion but from fear, as well. The storm had materialized so quickly with a ferociousness that was frightening. It was like a wild beast intent on attacking, swooping down and devouring them.

"There it is," Dakota shouted above the cacophony.

The rock shelter built by nature's hand was about five feet across and high, and six feet deep. They bent over and hurried under the protection, moving as far back as possible before turning and sinking to the dry ground.

Kathy gasped for breath, waiting for the burning in her lungs to dissipate. Dakota propped the Dream Catcher carefully against the side wall.

"The Dream Catcher is wet," he said, "but none of the webbing is damaged. If the wind shifts, we'll be pelted with rain, but at least we're in no danger from the lightning."

Kathy nodded, then pulled up her knees and wrapped her arms around them. A shiver coursed through her.

Dakota put one arm around her shoulders. "Are you cold, Kathy? The temperature has dropped more than twenty degrees, I imagine."

"Yes, it's chilly," she said, "but I'm scared, too. It was so peaceful, Dakota, with birds singing, squirrels chattering to one another, the leaves of the trees rustling gently when a breeze feathered them. Then . . . I don't know. The storm is ominous, a bleak, dark message of some kind."

"No," he said, then kissed her on the temple. "There's nothing to be frightened of. This is a typical storm in the Chiricahua Mountains. I've sought shelter right here in this cave countless times and waited for the weather to clear. I won't let anything happen to you, Kathy."

She turned to meet his gaze, then snuggled closer to him, resting her head on his shoulder. They watched the storm rage beyond the opening of the little cave.

Her fear, Kathy realized, was gone. She was with Dakota, and they were in a dry cocoon where no harm could touch them.

The storm had appeared out of nowhere, it seemed. It had just suddenly been there, not to be ignored. It wasn't ominous, it was symbolic. Dakota, too, had entered her existence with a dramatic and unexpected arrival. And Dakota most definitely could not be ignored.

The rain that now fell, she mused, would nurture the trees, grass, flowers and animals. It would provide what they needed in order to flourish as they were meant to. Dakota's emergence into her life had nurtured *her,* as well, made it possible for her to grow, achieve the maximum potential of her femininity, be all that she was capable of being as a woman.

She shifted her gaze to the Dream Catcher, seeing that it was slowly drying and returning to its soft-pink color. It was still two feet wide, as it had been when they left Douglas that morning.

It was so delicate, she thought, such a beautiful handmade creation. Yet the powers it possessed were almost beyond the scope of her imagination. It was shrouded in mystery and held the keys to the doors of life or death for Dakota.

And it was *her* fault that it was shrinking.

Kathy sighed, a sad-sounding sigh, then looked again at the pouring rain coming down in near-solid sheets.

Somewhere out there was the shaman, the only one who could turn the key to the proper door and make it possible for Dakota to stay in this time.

They would find the shaman.

Wouldn't they?

Twelve

During the next hour the rain began to slacken, finally diminishing to a fine mist. It was not as dark, nor as cold, and thunder no longer rolled across the heavens.

"We'd better leave," Dakota said. "We're still going to get wet, but that can't be avoided. The danger from the lightning is over, though. We'll have to move slower because everything will be slippery."

"What if we can't find the shaman before nightfall?" Kathy said, a slightly frantic edge to her voice. "What will we do then?"

"Don't worry about what hasn't yet happened, Kathy."

"Mmm," she said, glaring at him.

They left the cave, and Dakota filled his lungs with the fresh scent of rain, savoring it. While he indulged in nature's wonders, Kathy wistfully envisioned a warm bubble bath followed by deliciously dry, soft clothes.

With the Dream Catcher tucked securely beneath Dakota's arm, they started off.

Three hours went by without Kathy having to ask to rest, clearly indicating to her how slowly they were moving. The rain had stopped, their clothes had dried stiff as boards, but the temperature remained mercifully cool.

In the late afternoon they ate the energy protein bars they'd tucked into their pockets, washing them down with the tepid water in the sports bottles.

They continued on, and Dakota reached down yet again to extend his hand to Kathy to assist her to the top of the rock where he stood. When she was next to him, he swept one arm in the air.

"Down there," he said, "is the canyon we've been looking for."

"It is? All I can see are tops of trees and a whole bunch of very big boulders."

"If the shaman exists, as some people believe, he'll be in that canyon."

"*Some* people believe?" Kathy said. "*We* believe he's there."

Dakota stared at the area below.

"Dakota? You *do* believe that, don't you?"

Without speaking, he turned and walked away. Kathy sighed and trudged after him, deciding she just didn't have the energy to argue the point. She was thoroughly exhausted and had to concentrate on putting one foot in front of the other.

It took nearly an hour to weave their way down the rocky slope to the floor of the canyon. Kathy was nearly numb with fatigue, but was aware of the icy fingers of fear that were inching around her heart and mind.

This was it, she thought, staring at the mass of trees before her. The shaman was in there. Somewhere. He was. He had to be.

Dakota went forward and Kathy followed him, frowning at his broad back as he made a narrow path through the thick foliage.

Something was wrong, she thought. Dakota hadn't spoken to her since they'd seen the canyon from the top of the ridge. It was as though he'd withdrawn and erected an invisible barrier between them. She felt alone and lonely, and very, very frightened.

It was hot in the midst of the dense trees and extremely humid. A branch tangled in Kathy's curls, and she yanked it free, pulling painfully on her hair. Tears filled her eyes, and she had to struggle not to wail at full volume.

She was hot and tired. Her clothes were scratchy against her skin. She was scared, lonely, and Dakota was being as comforting as one of the unyielding rocks they'd been battling all day.

She wanted to go home, have a bubble bath, a good long cry, and be finished with this awful nightmare. She'd drag Dakota out of there by the back of the shirt and tell him in no uncertain terms that enough was enough. She'd fall madly in love with him and they'd live happily ever after. The end.

A wobbly little sob escaped from her throat.

That was what she wanted, but it wasn't remotely close to reality. If they didn't find the shaman, Dakota was going to die. It was too much to handle, all of it.

Two tears slid down her cheeks, followed by two more, and she sniffled. A few feet ahead of her, Dakota stopped, and she dashed the tears from her cheeks.

"What . . ." she started to say.

"Shh," he said, raising one hand but not turning to look at her.

She glowered at him, which didn't make her feel one bit better.

"The shaman," Dakota said, his voice low. "The shaman is here."

Kathy's eyes widened, and she hurried to stand next to Dakota, looking up at him eagerly.

"He is?" She glanced around. "Where? I don't see anything, anyone. How do you know he's here?"

"Shh."

"Darn it, Dakota, don't you dare tell me to be quiet," she said, none too quietly. "I've been in this frightening mess with you every inch of the way, and you're suddenly treating me as though I'm as unimportant as one of those crummy trees. Talk...to...me."

He looked down at her and narrowed his eyes. "Shh."

That did it.

Kathy burst into tears.

Dakota blinked, opened his mouth, shut it again, then frowned. Kathy covered her face with her hands and wept. He set the Dream Catcher against the trunk of a tree, then wrapped his arms around Kathy, holding her tightly to him.

"I'm sorry," he said gently. "I turned inward, attempting to control my fear and the pain I feel when I realize I might have to leave you, that I might die, and you'll be alone, crying. I centered on myself and I'm sorry."

Kathy tilted her head back to look at him. He raised one hand to wipe the tears from her face.

"It just all caught up with me," she said, her voice trembling. "I'm so tired, and so scared and... Oh, dear

God, Dakota, I don't want to lose you. Is the shaman really here? How do you know?"

"I sense his presence. I feel his power. He's very near."

She stepped back out of his embrace. "Then let's find him, let's hurry. Get the Dream Catcher and..." She looked at the base of the tree. "No! Oh, no. Dakota, the Dream Catcher...the Dream Catcher... No!"

He spun around and snatched it up.

It was only one foot wide.

Dakota grabbed Kathy's hand and began to move through the trees again, Kathy having to scramble to keep up with him. Ten minutes later with no warning, they suddenly emerged from the thick growth into a small clearing about the size of Kathy's living room. They stopped dead in their tracks.

The shaman.

He was sitting cross-legged on the ground behind a low-burning campfire. Clad in buckskin pants and shirt, he wore his gray hair in two heavy braids that hung to the middle of his chest. His face was a deep bronze, partly from heritage, but also from years spent in the sun. His skin was a mass of wrinkles, his age undeterminable, but he was obviously very old. His dark eyes met Dakota's.

"You have come, Dakota," the shaman said.

"I have come, mighty shaman," Dakota said.

"Dear heaven," Kathy whispered, tightening her hold on Dakota's hand.

"Sit," the shaman said. "Your woman may share my fire, as well."

They moved forward, and Kathy sank gratefully to the ground, her legs refusing to hold her for another moment. Her heart was racing as she stared at the shaman.

"I have waited for you, Dakota," the shaman said. "You have been honored, chosen, by the mystical powers of the Dream Catcher. It holds the ability to send you to your eternal beyond. Are you prepared to die, Dakota?"

"Yes."

"No," Kathy said. "Please. No. Can't you help us? Don't you know the answer to the mystery of the Dream Catcher? Can't you bring Dakota's center spirit here to him, so he can stay with me?"

"Tell your woman," the shaman said, still looking at Dakota, "that she may share my fire but she is not to speak."

Dakota squeezed Kathy's hand. "I have told her."

Kathy sighed.

The shaman frowned. "She should not have spoken, but I heard her words. Do you wish to stay in this era, Dakota? It is not yours. You don't belong here."

"It *is* mine now, the place where I belong," he said. "There is nothing left for me in my own time. My people have gone to the reservation, but I refused to go."

"Bronco Apache," the shaman said.

"Yes. This woman is my wife. I wish to remain with her. My spirit flows from my body. My center spirit did not travel with me through the Dream Catcher. I must be united with the center of my spirit, or I will die. Time is very short. I feel the weakness. The Dream Catcher is growing smaller."

"I know most of what you're telling me," the shaman said. "I saw the visions in the smoke of my fire. What I did *not* learn from the smoke pictures was that you wished to stay in this time."

"That is my wish."

"Mmm," the shaman said, shifting his gaze to stare at the fire.

Please, Kathy silently begged. *Oh, please.*

Several long minutes passed, then the shaman looked at Dakota again.

"All is not as it should be," the old man said. "The Dream Catcher diminishes in size because your woman is troubled. She is afraid and does not listen to the voices of her heart." He shifted his gaze to look directly into Kathy's eyes. "Perhaps you should give thought to what you've learned, as Dakota told you. I heard the echo of his words. They are wise. Turn inward, Dakota's woman, seek the truth. Then you may speak."

Kathy's heart raced, and another chill of fear swept throughout her. She wanted to run as fast and as far as she could, but she was held immobile by the mesmerizing dark eyes of the shaman.

Then slowly, slowly, a calmness settled over her, a sense of peace like nothing she'd experienced before. The chill was replaced by a warmth that suffused her, moving through her like a gentle whisper caressing her heart, mind, her very soul.

The voices in her mind that had plagued her with confusion, doubt and fear, quieted, then were still. She heard only one message that was clear, and rich and real.

She was in love with Dakota.

And Kathy Maxwell was filled with the greatest joy she had ever known.

"I was afraid," she said softly. "My fear of the risks of loving spoke in a voice louder than that of my heart. I used the differences in my world and Dakota's as a shield to protect myself. But now I know, believe, that we can overcome any obstacles in our path as long as we stand together, united. One."

She turned to meet Dakota's gaze.

"I love you, Dakota," she whispered. "I love you so very much, with all that I am as your wife."

"And I love you, Kathy, with all that I am as your husband."

She smiled at him warmly, gently, with love shining in the sky-blue depths of her eyes. It was a purely feminine smile of a woman grown. Understanding, glorying in the knowledge and rejoicing in its gifts.

"It is good," the shaman said, nodding. "You are now one, as it should be."

"I wish to stay in this time with my wife," Dakota said, looking at the shaman again.

"My father was a shaman," the old man said, staring into the fire, "as was his father, and the fathers for countless generations that came before. The teachings were passed from father to son, as is our Apache custom. The Dream Catcher has always been held in high esteem, for its powers are great." He paused. "I have never performed the ceremony of the Dream Catcher."

Kathy stiffened in fear, but Dakota slid her a quick glance, cautioning her with his eyes to keep silent.

No, no, no, her mind screamed. She loved Dakota. She was deeply in love with him, she knew that now. They couldn't have come all this way, actually found the shaman when no one else had been able to, only to discover that he didn't have the answer. That he didn't know the mystery of the Dream Catcher. *No! Dakota was not going to die.*

"You haven't performed the ceremony of the Dream Catcher," Dakota said, "but was it taught to you by your father?"

The shaman nodded.

Hope surged within Kathy.

The shaman met Dakota's gaze again. "It was taught to me, but..." He shook his head. "It was believed that if someone was touched by the Dream Catcher's powers and was hurled through time into the future, they would wish to return to where they belonged. The ceremony is for that purpose."

"You are very wise, mighty shaman," Dakota said. "Don't you possess the knowledge to reverse the ceremony? To bring my center spirit to me here?"

"I don't know. The risks are many. The ceremony is ancient, sacred. To tamper with what has always been might result in your death. I can be certain of nothing."

"I hear your words," Dakota said. "I would speak with my wife."

The shaman nodded and raised one hand in dismissal.

Dakota got to his feet, pulled Kathy to hers, and they moved to the edge of the clearing. He placed his hands on her shoulders and looked directly into her blue eyes, seeing the tears shimmering there.

"You've heard the shaman's words, Kathy," he said quietly.

"Yes," she said, tears echoing in her voice. "It's perfectly clear, Dakota. You must go back to your own time. It's too dangerous to attempt to reverse the ceremony. I love you too much to have you run that risk." Her breath caught on a sob. "You have to go back."

"No."

"But..."

"Listen to me," he said, tightening his hold on her shoulders. "*You* are here. *You* are my life. If I go back, Kathy, I would have nothing. Oh, yes, I'd be alive, but would I? Really? It would be a living death. Empty.

Lonely. Cold. I'm going to ask the shaman to attempt to reverse the ceremony of the Dream Catcher.''

Kathy grabbed the front of his shirt. ''You might die. He said that. You might die, Dakota.'' Tears streamed down her face. ''I don't want...don't want...you...to die.''

He pulled her close, resting one cheek on the top of her head.

''Would you wish me to go back to a world so empty, Kathy, that I can feel the pain of it by merely envisioning it in my mind?''

''No, but...''

''Kathy, I must do everything possible to stay here with you. I must. Now, hear me as I tell you what *you* must do. If...if I die, you will cry tears of healing to soothe the sadness of your spirit. Then you'll stand tall, proud, befitting the widow of an Apache brave who has gone to his eternal beyond.

''And, Kathy? Just as when my people did not look back upon what had been when they left the reservation, you will look only to the future. If I die, you will live on with dignity. You'll open your heart, your center spirit, to love, to laughter, to life. Do you understand?''

''Dakota, please, I can't...''

''Do you hear my words, Kathy?''

She nodded, feeling as though her heart was shattering into a million pieces.

''Come. We mustn't show a lack of respect by keeping the shaman waiting. I love you, Kathy Maxwell.''

''I love you,'' she whispered. *Forever. Only you. For all time.* ''I love you, Dakota Smith.''

They returned to sit in their places opposite the shaman. The old man looked at Dakota.

"It is my humble wish," Dakota said, "that you perform the ceremony of the Dream Catcher in reverse, mighty shaman. I honor and respect my wife. I love her and she loves me. We are one, united, until death and the eternal beyond separates us. I would stay in this world with her. I understand and accept the risks involved in what I am asking of you."

The shaman nodded. "So be it. You have decided on the proper course, Dakota, the one befitting a true Apache. To desert your wife because it would be of lesser risk to you has no honor. If you die because of your choice of action, your memory can be held in high esteem by your widow who shall weep."

"Mmm," Dakota said.

No! Kathy thought. Dakota was *not* going to die. She felt so helpless, so useless. There was nothing she could do but sit silently by and watch the events unfold. *Oh, Dakota.*

"We must go to the stream that runs past this enclosure," the shaman said. "There we will be in harmony with earth, air and water." He got to his feet. "Bring the Dream Catcher."

The shaman walked slowly but steadily, his firm step one of a much younger man.

They went around the end of the boulders edging the small canyon, then moved again through tall trees. A few minutes later they emerged to find a stream of crystal-clear water that flowed lazily over a bed of rocks. Lush grass grew on both sides of the stream.

"Wild raspberries," Dakota said, pointing across the brook. "They grew here when I was a boy and still flourish. I would come here, eat my fill of berries, drink the cool water, then lie in the grass and watch the clouds make pictures in the sky. I was at peace here."

"It's beautiful," Kathy said softly. "I can see you in my mind's eye coming here as you must have been as a boy. It *is* very peaceful."

The shaman went to a spot beyond the grassy section and made a small circle of rocks. Within minutes, a fire glowed in the center.

Dusk was beginning to fall, and a sunset was streaking across the sky in vibrant colors, casting a golden hue over the area. The shaman motioned for Dakota and Kathy to sit across from him, the circle of rocks separating them.

"Give me the Dream Catcher," the shaman said. "Do not touch your woman, nor is she to touch you. Turn into yourself, Dakota. Focus on the place within you that is empty, where the center of your spirit must come. See it. Feel it. Will it to return to you. I go now to my altered state. What happens beyond this moment is not under my control."

Dakota draped his hands on his knees as Kathy had seen him do many times in her backyard. He closed his eyes.

Wait! she thought frantically. *Please! Wait!* She wanted to hold him one more time. Kiss him one more time. Declare her love one more time.

But it was too late.

The shaman sat as Dakota did, the Dream Catcher on the ground in front of him. His eyes were closed as he took three deep breaths, releasing each through an open mouth.

Kathy jerked in surprise as the shaman began to chant in low, rumbling tones, the sounds having no discernible meaning to her.

Then slowly, slowly, a funnel of smoke began to swirl from the small fire, growing bigger and denser with every beat of Kathy's racing heart.

A gasp escaped from her lips as she stared at the spiraling smoke with wide eyes.

Forms were taking shape within the funnel. She could see them! She saw Dakota's face, and hers, then the image of the Dream Catcher became clear. The funnel moved, thicker, darker. The images vanished as the funnel encased Dakota in its depths until she could no longer see him. The shaman chanted on, louder now, the cadence faster.

Kathy was frozen in fear, unable to move, hardly able to breathe.

Dakota! her mind screamed. *Dakota! I love you. Stay with me. Bring your center spirit to you here. Here, Dakota. Don't leave. Don't go back in time. Stay. Stay, my love. Dakota . . . Dakota . . . Dakota . . .*

The smoke continued to whip around Dakota, then the top of the funnel grew and flung itself over the shaman, the Dream Catcher and the circle of rocks. It was only inches from Kathy, but didn't touch her.

She was alone and terrified outside the thick, spiraling wall of darkening smoke. She could no longer hear the shaman's chant, the only sound a humming noise created by the smoke funnel.

Time lost meaning.

Tears streamed unnoticed down Kathy's face. Her mind echoed Dakota's name over and over.

Dakota . . . Dakota . . . Dakota . . .

The smoke became dark as night. Churning. Swirling. Humming.

Dakota . . . Dakota . . . Dakota . . .

Suddenly Kathy felt as though she'd been struck by a powerful force that knocked her over, flat on her back on the ground. She struggled for air as black dots danced before her eyes. A wave of dizziness washed over her, and she closed her eyes, still gasping, trying to breathe.

She slipped away... into oblivion.

Kathy stirred and opened her eyes, blinking in confusion as she stared up at a night sky that twinkled with the diamondlike lights of a million stars. The brilliance of the heavens cast a silvery luminescence that was nearly as bright as day.

Where was she? What...

Dakota!

She scrambled to her knees, her heart beating so wildly it was actually painful.

Dakota was on the ground near her, his eyes closed. The shaman, the Dream Catcher and the circle of rocks were gone. There was no visible evidence that a fire had ever burned there.

"Dakota," she whispered.

She moved quickly to kneel beside him, placing her hands on his rugged cheeks, willing him to open his eyes. She moved one hand to his chest, rejoicing in the feel of his steady heartbeat beneath her palm.

"Dakota," she said, then increased the volume of her voice. "Dakota, it's Kathy. Wake up, my love. I'm here, waiting for you. Please, Dakota, please come to me. Dakota?"

He slowly opened his eyes, then drew a deep breath that shuddered through his body.

"Kathy?"

"Yes," she said, smiling even as tears filled her eyes. "Yes."

He struggled to sit up, took another deep breath, then shook his head slightly to clear it. He glanced around.

"The shaman?" he said.

"He's gone. The Dream Catcher is gone, too, and the rocks by the fire. Oh, Dakota, what happened? I was so frightened. There was a funnel of smoke that covered you, and I couldn't see you, or the shaman. I think I fainted, but I'm not sure. Do you remember anything?"

"I was...I was above the earth, being pulled in two directions at once. There was pain, intense pain, as though I was being torn apart. Images were everywhere. I saw my people, the soldiers, then you, your house, then back again to my people.

"But then... Yes, I heard your voice calling to me. Over and over you said my name, begging me to stay, to bring my center spirit here, to this time and place. I clung to your words like they were tangible objects. I held fast, endured the pain and refused to release my hold. Because of you and your love for me, Kathy, I'm here."

"Oh, Dakota," she said, dashing the tears from her cheeks. She paused and her eyes widened. "Your center spirit. Is it with you? How will we know if the ceremony really worked?"

Dakota frowned, then looked at the stream. "The truth can be learned if I look in the water."

"Your reflection," she whispered. "We couldn't see you in the mirror in my bedroom because you didn't have the center of your spirit."

"Yes. Go stand by the stream, Kathy, and look at your reflection. The stars will make it bright enough for you to see yourself. I'll join you in a moment, and we'll learn the truth of what has taken place."

"What are you going to do here while I go to the stream?"

"I must give humble thanks and say farewell to the shaman."

"Where did he go?"

"I don't know. His powers are far greater than anything I can understand. I now believe that no one else ever saw him because he wasn't here until we came, until we needed him. He won't return to this place. Ever."

"He took the Dream Catcher."

"Mmm," he said, nodding. "If my center spirit isn't within me, there's no more to be done. The Dream Catcher has no further purpose now. Go to the stream, Kathy." He brushed his lips over hers. "Go."

On trembling legs, Kathy did as Dakota had instructed her. At the edge of the stream, she stared at her reflection, which was clearly visible in the sparkling, silver-toned water. She wrapped shaking hands around her elbows.

And waited.

Her heart pounded and her throat ached.

She waited.

Within minutes she would learn what the future held.

She waited . . . for what seemed like an eternity.

Then . . .

Dakota!

His reflection was there in the water as he came to stand behind her. He lifted his hands to place them on her shoulders, and she felt his warm, gentle touch at the same glorious moment it was mirrored in the stream.

She spun to face him and flung her arms around his neck, crying openly with joy. He held her tightly to him, tears streaming down his cheeks, as well. They rocked back and forth, saying each other's names, happiness dispelling the lingering shadows of fear within them.

Then Dakota sought and found her mouth, kissing her deeply, urgently. Desire rocketed through them, their passion as hot as the flames of the fire the shaman had built in the circle of rocks.

"Kathy," Dakota said, close to her lips. "I want to make love with you here, by this stream that has told us we're to spend the remainder of our lives together."

"Yes. Oh, yes, my love."

They shed their clothes quickly, each appearing to the other like an exquisite statue crafted from fine silver. And there on the plush grass they joined, meshed their bodies, were one.

It was ecstasy.

It was the beginning of their forever.

Afterward they lay close, entwined, listening to the lilting song sung by the gentle ripple of the brook.

Dakota splayed one hand on Kathy's stomach, then shifted up to rest on one forearm so he could look directly into her eyes.

"Kathy, my wife, you have conceived my son on this night. He rests here, within you, beneath my palm."

"I ... Your son? Are you sure?"

Dakota nodded. "You carry my son. Are you upset, unhappy, that this has happened?"

"Oh, no, Dakota, no. It's wonderful. I'll be very proud to bear your child, Dakota. It's perfect, so special, that he was conceived here in this place. Thank you, Dakota. Oh, how I love you."

"And I love you."

He kissed her, then they settled again in the soft grass, both realizing how exhausted they were from the incredible events that had transpired.

"We'll spend the night here in nature's bed," Dakota said. "In the morning we'll feast on wild raspberries and drink the clear water of the stream.

"Then, Kathy, we'll leave the Chiricahua Mountains for the last time. I'll never return. My life as I knew it here is over. The now and the future are of importance, not the past. Our son may wish to see this place some day, but that will be his choice to make."

"Yes, my love," Kathy said. She snuggled closer to him and placed one hand on her stomach with a sense of wonder and infinite joy. "In the morning we'll go home, together." She smiled. "The three of us."

Epilogue

Kathy stood in front of the full-length mirror in Lily and Brad's bedroom and stared at her own reflection.

She was wearing a white gauze dress with a scooped neckline that came to just above her breasts and stopped at the edges of her shoulders. Bright wildflowers had been embroidered across the bodice and on the wide border of the street-length hem. It was nipped in at the waist with a gauze belt.

It was a lovely dress, beautiful in its simplicity.

It was her wedding dress.

Kathy smiled, a soft, gentle smile, as she splayed both hands on her flat stomach. Love for the baby being nurtured there, the child created by the meshing of Kathy's body with Dakota's, suffused her.

"Your father and I became husband and wife according to the customs of his people," she whispered to the baby. "Now we'll be married by the rituals set forth by mine. Both of those worlds will be yours to discover and rejoice in, little one. Oh, you are loved beyond measure already. You're a miracle and we'll cherish you."

"Kathy?"

She turned to see Lily in the doorway.

"Are you ready?" Lily said. "You look wonderful." She crossed the room to hug Kathy. "I'm so happy for you and Dakota."

"Thank you, Lily." Kathy smiled. "I'm happy for us, too."

"Here's your bouquet. Wildflowers, just like you wanted. The gazebo is threaded with wildflowers, too. Your parents and mine are beaming, as though they're taking credit for you and Dakota being together. They adore your man, you realize."

"Well, they might be a tad nervous if we'd told them the truth about how he came into my life," Kathy said, laughing. "Parents don't have to know everything."

"Amen to that," Lily said. "Well, here we go, Mrs. Smith. You're about to become Mrs. Smith...again. This family-only ceremony is the final, perfect touch in blending your world with Dakota's. Oh-h-h, I'm going to weep through the whole thing, I just know I will." She threw up her hands and marched from the room.

Kathy followed more slowly, allowing a sense of peace and contentment to caress her mind and soul, while the love for Dakota nestled warmly around her heart.

When she stepped into the backyard, she didn't see the pretty gazebo with the minister standing inside, nor her parents and Lily's. She wasn't aware that Brad was holding a sleeping Michelle Dakota, or that the other three little girls were wiggling like excited puppies. Lily's sniffling into a lace-edged hankie didn't register.

She saw only Dakota.

He was dressed in a butter-soft, white doeskin shirt, pants and moccasins. Wildflowers were embroidered on the cuffs of the shirt. His shoulder-length hair gleamed like polished ebony in the sunlight.

She moved toward him, her gaze locked with his. She walked alone, not on the arm of her father as was more traditional. She'd gently explained to her dad that he really couldn't 'give her away,' because she belonged only to herself, was an entity unto herself.

"When did you become so wise?" he'd said, smiling at her.

"When I fell in love with Dakota."

Kathy came to the gazebo and smiled up at Dakota. He matched her smile, then they turned, went up the three steps, and crossed to stand in front of the minister.

"Friends," the clergyman said, "we have gathered here today as witnesses for Kathy and Dakota as they repeat the vows that will unite them as husband and wife."

The words flowed around Kathy as she looked directly into Dakota's eyes, seeing there all she needed to know, seeing there all she needed.

Time lost meaning, then suddenly Dakota was kissing her, they wore simple gold wedding bands, and everyone was hugging, or kissing, or shaking hands, with everyone else.

"I love you," Dakota said, close to her ear.

"I love you, too, but I sort of floated away during the ceremony. I missed the whole thing."

"Does it matter?"

"No. I'm your wife. I will love and cherish you until the day I die. We have a whole lifetime together to explore, Dakota."

"Discoveries," he said, nodding. "That has merit."

"Oh, I must show you something before we have cake and punch," Kathy's mother announced to the group. "I bought it yesterday at the craft show on the plaza, but we were so busy getting ready for the wedding that I forgot about it. It's fascinating and really very pretty."

She opened an enormous purse and withdrew a small tissue-wrapped package. Brushing back the paper, she held up her newly acquired, bright blue, three-inch-wide treasure.

"Isn't it lovely?" she said. "It's called a Dream Catcher. I'm going to hang it on the wall above my pillow when we return home to Florida. Don't you think that's a marvelous idea?"

"No!" Kathy, Dakota, Lily and Brad said in unison.

"Well, why on earth not?" she said, obviously confused.

Lily launched into a speech listing every reason imaginable why her aunt should hang the Dream Catcher in the kitchen, because one generally didn't sleep, thus dream, in the said room.

"Dream Catchers *do* have merit," Kathy said to Dakota.

"Mmm," he said.

And then they smiled, love shining in their eyes.

* * * * *

FORTUNE'S Children™

In July, get to know the Fortune family....

Next month, don't miss the start of Fortune's Children, a fabulous new twelve-book series from Silhouette Books.

Meet the Fortunes—a family whose legacy is greater than riches. Because where there's a will...there's a wedding!

When Kate Fortune's plane crashes in the jungle, her family believes that she's dead. And when her will is read, they discover that Kate's plans for their lives are more interesting than they'd ever suspected.

Look for the first book, *Hired Husband*, by *New York Times* bestselling author **Rebecca Brandewyne.** PLUS, a stunning, perforated bookmark is affixed to *Hired Husband* (and selected other titles in the series), providing a convenient checklist for all twelve titles!

FREE
Keepsake
Bookmark

Launching in July wherever books are sold.

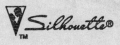
Silhouette®

One Western family finds the kind of love
that legends—and little ones—are made of....

It all starts with

THE COWBOY AND THE CRADLE
by bestselling author **Cait London**

It figures that the most wanted man in Wyoming has
sworn off ever getting married *or* making babies. But
according to family legend (and one very sexy single
mom) Duncan will soon be saying "I Do" and having a
houseful of baby Tallchiefs!

Book 1 of her heartwarming, sexy new miniseries is
available in June from Silhouette Desire—part of
Celebration 1000!

Look for Book 2 of **The Tallchiefs** miniseries,
Tallchief's Bride, as September's *Man of the Month,*
only in

CHIEFS

SILHOUETTE DESIRE® "CELEBRATION 1000" SWEEPSTAKES
OFFICIAL RULES—NO PURCHASE NECESSARY

To enter, complete an Official Entry Form or a 3"x5" card by hand printing "Silhouette Desire Celebration 1000 Sweepstakes," your name and address, and mail it to: In the U.S.: Silhouette Desire Celebration 1000 Sweepstakes, P.O. Box 9069, Buffalo, NY 14269-9069, or In Canada: Silhouette Desire Celebration 1000 Sweepstakes, P.O. Box 637, Fort Erie, Ontario L2A 5X3. Limit one entry per envelope. Entries must be sent via first-class mail and be received no later than 6/30/96. No liability is assumed for lost, late or misdirected mail.

Prizes: Grand Prize—an original painting (approximate value $1500 U.S.);300 Runner-up Prizes—an autographed Silhouette Desire® Book (approximate value $3.50 U.S./$3.99 CAN. each). Winners will be selected in a random drawing (to be conducted no later than 9/30/96) from among all eligible entries received by D.L. Blair, Inc., an independent judging organization whose decision is final.

Sweepstakes offer is open only to residents of the U.S. (except Puerto Rico) and Canada who are 18 years of age or older, except employees and immediate family members of Harlequin Enterprises Ltd., their affiliates, subsidiaries, and all agencies, entities and persons connected with the use, marketing or conduct of this sweepstakes. All federal, state, provincial, municipal and local laws apply. Offer void where prohibited by law. Taxes and/or duties are the sole responsibility of the winners. Any litigation within the province of Quebec respecting the conduct and awarding of prizes may be submitted to the Regie des alcools des courses et des jeux. All prizes will be awarded; winners will be notified by mail. No substitution for prizes is permitted. Odds of winning are dependent upon the number of eligible entries received.

Grand Prize winner must sign and return an Affidavit of Eligibility within 30 days of notification. In the event of noncompliance within this time period, prize may be awarded to an alternate winner. Any prize or prize notification returned as undeliverable may result in the awarding of that prize to an alternate winner. By acceptance of their prize, winners consent to the use of their names, photographs or likenesses for purposes of advertising, trade and promotion on behalf of Harlequin Enterprises Ltd., without further compensation unless prohibited by law. In order to win a prize, residents of Canada will be required to correctly answer a time-limited arithmetical skill-testing question administered by mail.

For a list of winners (available after October 31, 1996) send a separate self-addressed stamped envelope to: Silhouette Desire Celebration 1000 Sweepstakes Winners, P.O. Box 4200, Blair, NE 68009-4200.

SWEEPR

"Motherhood is full of love, laughter and sweet surprises. Silhouette's collection is every bit as much fun!"
—Bestselling author Ann Major

This May, treat yourself to...

WANTED:

Silhouette's annual tribute to motherhood takes a new twist in '96 as three sexy single men prepare for fatherhood—and saying "I Do!" This collection makes the perfect gift, not just for moms but for all romance fiction lovers! Written by these captivating authors:

Annette Broadrick
Ginna Gray
Raye Morgan

"The Mother's Day anthology from Silhouette is the highlight of any romance lover's spring!"
—Award-winning author **Dallas Schulze**

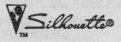